SCANDAL AT THE GALA

A SWEETFERN HARBOR MYSTERY #8

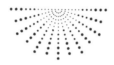

WENDY MEADOWS

MAJESTIC
OWL
PUBLISHING LLC

CHAPTER ONE

GALA PREPARATION

*S*heffield Bed and Breakfast buzzed with excitement when owner Brenda Rivers told her employees about the invitation. The local hospital had asked her to plan and host a fundraiser for cancer research, working toward a cure. Brenda's pleasure heightened at the responses she received.

"I've been given the option to come up with a theme, or else the hospital can provide one," Brenda said. "I have a few ideas of my own. What do you guys think about a masquerade gala?"

"That's a great idea," Phyllis said. Brenda's best friend and head housekeeper spoke, just before Allie had a chance to say the same thing. "It will be a fun celebration while raising money for a cause everyone can get behind. I'll ask William for a list of wealthy people he knows."

Her husband, William Pendleton, was well-known in successful business circles. Some of his friends had careers in the arts or theater, and others in banking or other industries. Brenda agreed it was a perfect idea.

"If we do a good job, maybe we can do this event every year," Allie said. The young reservationist glowed with excitement, her eyes sparkled as ideas ran through her head. "I'll come up with a design for the invitations if you want me to, Brenda."

"While you're at it, think about decorations for the gala itself," Brenda told her.

Allie Williams was known around Sweetfern Harbor as a budding artist. Her talent showed at every special event around town in her posters or paintings. She was Brenda's youngest employee and had a winning way with every guest that walked through the door.

"I'll call the shops down on Main Street and warn them they'll need to stock lots of masks for the masquerade night." Brenda paused, "Now, isn't there some sort of antique shop in town that sells old costumes, too?"

"Yes, Shakespeare's Attic," Allie said, with mounting excitement. "I've seen everything there from flapper dressers from Roaring Twenties, to Victorian ball gowns."

"And don't forget those trunks of costumes and masks your Uncle Randolph stored in the attic," Phyllis said. "I'll look through them in case some of our guests here

2

at the bed and breakfast don't have time to get their own."

Brenda immediately poured them all fresh cups of coffee or hot tea. They sat down at the long table in the kitchen, where they informed Chef Morgan of what was coming up next. Brenda told her they would get together in plenty of time to plan for the food and drink. "We'll have to mainly serve finger foods since everyone will be wearing masks," she said.

As they chattered away, Mac stuck his head in the doorway. "I wondered where everyone had gone," the detective said. He leaned over and kissed his wife. Brenda immediately felt herself in a different, more loving world at his touch. "What's going on?"

Brenda told him about the invitation to host the gala. It sounded to Mac as if they were already deep into the planning stage, but Phyllis assured him they were just beginning to plan. Mac groaned, shook his head and hid a smile as he left them. "I have to get on into the station. Good luck, ladies," he said as he left.

Only two hours later, the women gathered again to review ideas. Allie had designed a large planning chart and now spread it across the low table in the sitting room. All the guests had checked out except one couple. The women and the two remaining guests would dine together at noon. Once the couple left, Allie would be kept busy registering their new guests.

"We'd better take advantage of this down time while it lasts," Brenda said.

She bent over the chart and began filling in steps to take. She was interrupted by Allie, who suddenly stood up and snapped her fingers.

"I have it," she said. "Why not have a color theme for the event?" Brenda encouraged her to continue. "The invitations could request black and white attire only, with masks of gold or silver if they want variation."

The other two agreed it was a good idea. "Decorations should be black and white, too," Phyllis said. Brenda suggested the flowers be white, and maybe Jenny could insert smaller buds using minor accent colors in jewel tones, emphasizing the opulent nature of the gala.

"I can stop at Jenny's Blossoms after lunch and talk it over with her," Phyllis said. "I'll tell William to meet me at Morning Sun Coffee and we can talk about guests."

Jenny Rivers Jones was newly married to Detective Bryce Jones, and had become Brenda's step daughter a few months earlier when Brenda had married Mac. Jenny's Blossoms sold only high quality blooms and arrangements, and Brenda knew she could count on Jenny to come up with some great floral ideas for the gala's theme. Allie left them to check the names of the next arrivals due at the bed and breakfast. Phyllis joined Brenda in the dining room where they greeted the remaining couple for lunch. Still excited about the upcoming event, Brenda invited them to come back to Sweetfern Harbor the weekend of the big gala. She apologized that the Sheffield Bed and Breakfast's rooms had been booked long before the hospital asked her to host the fundraiser that particular weekend.

"If you think you'd like to come back for the event, you might want to book a hotel while you're still in town. Once the invitations go out, rooms in town will probably fill up fast." The couple agreed they would think about that before leaving.

When Brenda finished her lunch, she went to the front desk and told Allie she would watch for anyone arriving early while Allie took a lunchbreak, though Allie was still eager to discuss the upcoming event.

"March is a good time to have a break like a masquerade party," she said. "Everyone is looking forward to spring again and we all need a party."

Brenda agreed and reminded her to take her chance now to get some food. After Allie left, Brenda looked over the list of guests who would soon arrive. Everything had been checked over twice, as was the standard that she required. The rooms were spotless and inviting. Another week of guests filled the reservation list. Brenda scanned the computer for the guest roster for the weekend of the gala. She didn't recognize any of the names. They were all in for a treat when they realized they would be at the Sheffield for such a fancy party.

"I'm going to Jenny's to check on flower arrangements," Phyllis called to Brenda. "Do you need anything from downtown?"

Brenda told her she didn't encouraged her to enjoy some time with her daughter while she was out. Molly Lindsey owned Morning Sun Coffee, a favorite gathering place for townspeople and tourists alike, including her parents Phyllis and William.

When Allie returned to the desk, she was still full of enthusiasm and immediately started sketching ideas for the invitations. Once Brenda had William's list plus her own, invitations would be mailed out. They decided to limit the number of attendees to one hundred, plus an extra seven spots in case there were any last-minute invitations to be sent.

"That extra seven should cover anyone William or I come up with," Brenda said. "I have no idea how many he will think of, but I'll get the list from him no later than tomorrow. That will give everyone a month to prepare." She looked at the calendar. February was flying by and there was much to do. She told Allie she was going to her apartment to make some calls. "I need to set up a meeting with the hospital coordinator to let her know what we're thinking and make sure we've got the go ahead."

On her way upstairs, Brenda listed in her mind the many tasks to be done in order to pull off an impressive masquerade gala. Lighting must be spectacular to bring out the mystery of the entire atmosphere. She knew she could count on Jenny to take care of the bouquets, and Allie to come up with creative designs for décor and invitations. She would meet with her chef later in the afternoon to plan out the menu. Hope Williams, Allie's mother and owner of Sweet Treats, had already promised to present dessert ideas to Brenda the next day.

As it turned out, the hospital event coordinator was thrilled with their plans and Brenda was able to work everything out with her over the phone, saving time. Afterward, she called Hope right away to see if they could move up their visit, and Hope told her to come on down.

Welcoming Brenda into Sweet Treats with a warm smile, Hope already had several dessert samples ready to show her. Hope knew the desserts had to be small enough to be easily consumed because of the masks and style of the event. She invited Brenda to taste chocolate squares with a dollop of cream and raspberries on top. The treats were not as heavily laden with toppings as usual, just enough to be colorful and taste delicious.

"Do you want a chocolate fountain?" Hope asked. "We could put an assortment of cheeses, crackers and fruit at the base."

"I love that idea. Could you add nuts, too? My chef is taking care of finger foods and your dessert ideas are perfect."

Brenda's cell rang just as she left Sweet Treats.

"I have a great idea for entertainment at your gala, Brenda," Bryce said. Brenda held her breath, all too aware of the young detective's wild taste in music. He had picked the music played for his Valentine's Day wedding to Jenny. "I promise it isn't as far out there as we had at the wedding," he teased.

"That's reassuring," Brenda said. "It can't appeal to only the younger crowd. We'll have many high society types there who are older, and I want to make a good impression while raising a lot of money for the cause."

By the time the conversation ended, Brenda was satisfied with Bryce's ideas. She told him she would give her final answer after he provided links for his choices of music. He agreed and told her she would not be disappointed. "The band I have in mind is popular with everyone."

As she passed Jenny's Blossoms, Brenda noticed her step-daughter in the window setting up a new display. She went inside to say hello.

"I just talked with Bryce. He has music ideas for my gala."

Jenny laughed, remembering how Brenda and her dad

reacted to their wedding music. "I'm sure you'll screen what he has picked out and tone it down a bit," Jenny said.

"You can be sure of that. I told him I don't want to run people off before they donate big bucks to the cause." Brenda admired Jenny's display. "We'll have a live band, and everyone will unveil themselves just before the last dance. Mac suggested we set up tables for cards, like poker, in the large sunroom off the sitting room. Everyone who plays would then donate their winnings. What do you think?"

"I think anything either of you comes up with will be perfect, but that is a good way to keep some people there, who might otherwise lose interest. Like a certain someone who suggested it. I'm getting excited about the whole affair, but still have to pick out the most mysterious masks for Bryce and me. I'm having my dress made down at My Heart Bridal Shop. I'm getting a discount since they made my wedding dress. I tried to get in line first so it would be finished in time."

Brenda and Phyllis had already decided to go through Randolph's trunks in the attic and hope for more than one choice of black and white gowns. "I'm going to stop at the Shakespeare's Attic antique shop to look over masks," Brenda said. "I think I'll call and see if Phyllis can join me so we can do it together." Brenda stopped herself and glanced at her watch. "I need to hurry along. I have lots to do before this entire event unfolds." Jenny reminded her just to ask if she thought of anything more she could do to help than figure the flowers out.

Phyllis was leaving her daughter's coffee shop and joined Brenda at the antique store. "The trunks in the attic are all pulled out, just waiting for us to pilfer through them for our attire."

After trying on numerous masks, they each made their choice and headed back to the bed and breakfast.

"It's almost time for our next guests to arrive," Brenda said. "Let's look in the trunks later."

Phyllis agreed and left Brenda to check on refreshments for the next arrivals. She loved going through Randolph Sheffield's theatrical paraphernalia every chance she got. The opportunity to wear one of the costumes was the icing on the cake for Phyllis.

The weeks flew by and the bed and breakfast buzzed in anticipation of the event. Allie had made a note that there were two sisters arriving from a small Massachusetts town. They had entered a contest at an antique shop in Stockbridge to win a weekend away at Sheffield Bed and Breakfast in Sweetfern Harbor. They won the promotion and Brenda looked forward to meeting them. With the gala coming up that weekend, they would arrive to enjoy it along with the usual sights and specialty shops downtown.

CHAPTER TWO

GUEST ARRIVALS

The days sped by until only two days were left before Brenda and her staff would pull off the biggest event yet for Sheffield Bed and Breakfast. Every invitation had been accepted, and as expected, William came up with five more last-minute invitees.

"I tried to think of everyone I could for you, Brenda. All will be generous, I'm sure," William said. "One of your guests is someone I knew a while back. He has always been a giving person in the past and I don't expect anything less for this event. His name is Matthew Thomason, he's in the textile business, and very wealthy. It's been quite a while since I've seen him in person so it will be good to reconnect."

Brenda thanked him for coming up with potential donors

so quickly, then William left to join his wife Phyllis, who was rearranging two vases on the mantle in the sitting room. He smiled when he saw her. Before he married her, he could never have imagined how happy his life would turn out in his sixties. They were like very young newlyweds and he cherished every moment with her. William had failed to convince Phyllis that he had enough money to support her without her continuing in her head housekeeper position at the bed and breakfast. Once he understood her passion for her work, and for everyone connected there, he accepted her choice. Both stayed busy and enjoyed evenings alone together. Phyllis still had an apartment at the bed and breakfast, where they planned to stay during the masquerade gala; otherwise they enjoyed the Pendleton mansion where William had lived for many years before they met.

Tim Sheffield walked through the door. "I thought you might have a job for me, Brenda." He looked fondly at his daughter. "I discovered some entertainment while traveling abroad." Brenda's looked at him with an expectant expression. "The Juggling Jacques are in Sweetfern Harbor practicing their street acts for celebrations this summer. I asked them if they would perform outside as the guests arrive on the night of the masquerade shindig. I hope you don't mind."

"That's a great idea, Dad. The guests will be loving it the minute they step from their cars, Where are they from?"

"I met them on the streets of Paris, and they are currently touring America. They agreed right away since it will be a chance for them to advertise their talents."

Father and daughter chatted a while longer. Phyllis greeted Tim and invited him for a cup of hot coffee, which he accepted. "I wonder if your chef has any of those specialty scones of hers made up," Tim mentioned, trying not to look too eager. Everyone at the bed and breakfast was well aware that the chef, Anna, was attracted to Brenda's father. Brenda thought she had observed some reciprocation on her father's part, too.

"If she doesn't," Phyllis said with a smile, "I'm sure, for you, she would whip some up right away."

Brenda looked over Allie's shoulder, reviewing the list to refresh her mind about the bed and breakfast guests. It appeared there would be a variety and she hoped they would prove compatible with one another, especially for conversations at mealtime. They ranged from the two sisters who won the weekend away, and a millionaire, or billionaire perhaps, with whom William was acquainted. There was also a young couple coming, plus other guests, all of whom expected to attend the masquerade party. A few knew of the event ahead of time; others did not, but would soon enough. There were so many details that Brenda's head fairly spun, but she was grateful for Allie and Phyllis and everyone else helping to make the event go smoothly.

Allie and Brenda glanced up as the foyer door swung open just then. A boyish-looking young man smiled broadly and balanced two large bags while standing back for a young woman to enter. She carried an overnight case and her purse. Both were in their twenties and very cheerful.

"Looks like we made it to the right place," he said to the young woman. She responded in the affirmative and laughed. "We're the McAuliffe's," he said. "I'm Jack and this is my wife Emily." He shifted the one bag he still held to the other hand and reached out and shook Brenda's hand.

"Welcome to Sheffield Bed and Breakfast," she said. "I hope you enjoy your stay with us."

Michael, the porter, stepped forward to take the bags.

"I don't mind carrying at least one of them," Jack said. "I'll spare you Emily's, since it wouldn't be good to cause you a back injury so soon after we arrived." Emily punched his shoulder playfully.

Brenda and Allie did not miss the fact that the couple traveled with expensive, designer luggage. The three made their way upstairs, Michael showing them to their room.

"She is so pretty," Allie said, her voice in a whisper. "Don't you love that long blonde hair and perfect complexion?"

14

Brenda agreed. "I'm sure we both noticed that Jack McAuliffe isn't so bad looking either."

Both women laughed softly. There was no more time for comments, as the next guests had arrived. Maddie Kemp appeared to be in her early to mid-thirties, and her sister Susan Wathen several years older. They stood just inside the foyer and gazed in wonder at the beauty of the Queen Anne architecture and various details and decor. Allie and Brenda waited for them to take it all in. Susan was first to realize they were gaping, and Maddie's eyes shined like crystals.

"It is all so beautiful," Maddie said. "I don't think I've ever been in a place like this. I'll have to keep pinching myself to remember I get to spend the whole weekend here."

They checked in and Michael appeared on cue, escorted them up the wide staircase. Both women held onto the railing to keep balanced while staring at the architecture and the stained-glass window on the landing.

"I hope we don't make fools of ourselves in such a beautiful place," Susan said as they stepped carefully on the antique stair carpet.

Maddie giggled, as Michael kept his eyes straight ahead and hid a smile.

There was one guest yet to arrive. Matthew Thomason had requested a late arrival and said not to hold dinner for him. A few hours later, everyone sat at the long dining room table for their first dinner together. Servers placed salads in front of guests and retreated to the buffet table where they prepared drinks of choice for everyone. Brenda, Mac, Phyllis and William joined the diners, and conversations flowed easily. Emily McAuliffe was enthralled with Maddie's story of how she and her sister chanced to win their weekend getaway.

"I simply walked into the little antique shop to look around. I'll admit I don't always have money to buy what I want when I want it." If nothing else, Maddie Kemp was open about her circumstances. "I was heading for the door when the clerk asked if I wanted to sign up to win a weekend away at Sheffield Bed and Breakfast in Sweetfern Harbor. I jumped at the chance. When I got home and called Susan to tell her, she scoffed at me for thinking I'd win." She turned to her sister who appeared to be signaling her to stop talking. Maddie picked up on the warning and her face flushed.

"Go on," Emily said. "When did you find out you won?"

Maddie immediately regained her enthusiasm. "About two weeks later, the shop owner called to tell me to come down and pick up the reservation. It was for two, so of course, I wanted Susan to come with me. We got together and decided on the weekend, and here we are."

"You planned to come for the masquerade gala then," Emily said.

Maddie and Susan looked blank. "Is that something going on in town this weekend?" Susan asked. Brenda explained the party would be held at Sheffield Bed and Breakfast. Several added comments and explanations. "I'm afraid we won't be able to attend," Maddie said, with some disappointment. "Neither of us brought anything appropriate for a gala, or anything black and white at all, for that matter."

Phyllis waved her hand. "Never mind that. Brenda's uncle, who once owned this establishment, was into theater. There are several trunks of costumes in the attic. First thing tomorrow morning we'll go upstairs and rummage through them. I'm sure there are plenty of ball gowns in black and white for you to choose from."

"Then it's settled," Emily said, smiling encouragingly at Maddie. "Jack and I still have to get masks. Why don't you two come with us to the shop downtown tomorrow and we'll all pick some out."

Maddie and Susan accepted the invitation, and Brenda could see from the excitement on their faces that the weekend was proving to be more than a mere getaway. After dinner, Brenda happened to overhear the sisters as they walked down the hall. Susan had pulled her billfold from her purse. "I wonder how much masks like that will cost?"

"I hadn't thought of that," Maddie said, in a hushed tone. "Do you think we have enough extra money for them?"

"We'll just sacrifice spending at the shops," her sister said with a sigh. "I think the gala will be a lot of fun. At least we won't have to buy dresses to wear. That would be out of our range for sure."

"I knew this would be a good thing for you, Susan. You've been so sad since Ben died in that accident. I hope this will lighten your spirits again." Susan nodded. As the two women turned the corner of the hall and went out of Brenda's sight, Brenda could see a kind of sadness in the older sister Susan, as if she had lost the love of her life. She was glad to know the sisters were determined to have fun, despite their circumstances.

Brenda and Mac sat together in the sitting room later that evening. Matthew Thomason was due to arrive any minute, and Mac had offered to sit with Brenda until he settled in. They talked about the upcoming event.

"I can't believe it's finally all coming together," Brenda said.

"I'm not surprised at all that you've managed so well. You're becoming expert at things like this." Mac pulled her closer for a kiss.

They were interrupted when the door into the foyer opened. Brenda went out to greet Matthew Thomason. He was rather thin and his shoulders stooped slightly, which caused him to look older than his fifty-one years.

He had driven up from New York City and Brenda decided he must have had a long work day before making the trip up. Greeting him, she checked him in on the computer system, and Mac offered to carry his bag up after he declined refreshments. Brenda locked the front door and followed them upstairs. Matthew was shown his room and Brenda told him about the amenities listed on the paper she handed him. She reminded him she was on the premises and to call her right away if he needed anything. Matthew nodded and attempted to send a weak, fatigued smile her way. Brenda and Mac left him, knowing their guest would sleep well that night.

Once in their apartment, Mac commented on how tired the man looked. Brenda agreed and both hoped their guest would feel better after a good night's sleep. "William will cheer him up. It's been a while since he's seen Matthew," Brenda said.

The next morning everyone gathered for breakfast around the same time. Allie was introduced to Matthew Thomason, the only guest she had not personally checked in. The lines around his eyes now appeared even deeper than the night before. Brenda made a mental note to inquire if his room was comfortable enough.

Mac went into the kitchen and drank coffee while munching a sweet roll made by the chef. He always preferred to eat in the kitchen in the mornings, rather than joining the guests in the dining room. He chatted with Chef Morgan and then hurried off to the police station for work.

After breakfast, Brenda nodded to Phyllis, who told Maddie and Susan to follow her to the attic. Once there, Phyllis told them a few stories about the history of the Sheffield Bed and Breakfast.

"Randolph Sheffield was the owner until Brenda took over. She is his niece and he left it to her in his will. He made the perfect choice. Brenda's father Tim lives in town and he and Randolph were brothers. This is a historic Queen Anne mansion, built in the late 1800s, and was lovingly restored by Randolph's own hands over the course of many years..."

Maddie and Susan hung on her every word. They showed special interest in the history of the bed and breakfast and Phyllis loved telling stories to the guests. When Phyllis opened up the antique steamer trunks filled with costumes, the sisters gasped with pleasure to see the satins and silks of the old costumes stored between layers of delicate tissue. Each woman tried on several possibilities before deciding. Maddie chose a sleek black dress with a narrow white trim around the scooped neckline. Susan's choice was one that had a voluminous, layered skirt in black and a bodice that sparkled with tiny rhinestones over white linen.

Maddie gushed her thanks to Phyllis. "There is no way

we could afford dresses like these. The fact they are from a real, historical theater production is even better," she said. In the dusty attic light they looked at the tags of the dresses, where the names of long-forgotten actresses and plays were sewn. Maddie's tag revealed tiny print, reading *V. Allen, Duchess of Malfi, Act III Scene ii*, and Susan's tag read only *Princess Mary*. "My sister and I will truly feel like royalty, you see," Maddie said, beaming at Phyllis.

Allie met them as they came downstairs. "My mother has a box filled with costume jewelry left to her by her own mother. There are several pieces that look like the real thing. I asked her if you could borrow some from her and she said yes. We've picked from them already but there are still some beautiful pieces left. She will deliver bagels in a little while and promised to bring it with her if you're interested."

"Everyone is so generous around here. Thank you," Susan said with eyes misted.

Allie hugged her. "Emily is waiting for you two to go to the Shakespeare's Attic antique shop for your masks. She's in the sitting room. I'll let my mother know you want to look over the jewelry and she can leave the box with me." They returned to their rooms to pick up their purses and jackets and quickly joined their new friend.

"Jack has opted out, saying he didn't want to spend all his time waiting for us to decide on everything we look at."

Emily stood up, giggling. "He really just doesn't want to put up with me and my shopping habits, plus he's more interested in sailing right now. We'll have a good time together and I'll get his mask for him."

The three left and started up a lively conversation on their way to the shop. In between telling the sisters about the extensive travels around the globe she had done with her husband, Emily mentioned Jack's love for sailing again and told them she doubted he would get much sailing in because of choppy waters. However, he would no doubt go inspect the yachts in their berths anyhow. She continued to talk of things neither sister had ever imagined in their lives.

Maddie asked how she met Jack. Emily said they met on a skiing trip in Vail, Colorado.

"That's so romantic," Maddie said. Emily agreed it had been.

She described the lodge they stayed in. Every detail mesmerized the sisters, who listened avidly until the trio arrived at the shop. One side of the shop contained a fascinating range of vintage and antique treasures, everything from cases of leather-bound books and gold opera glasses, to a massive old Victrola record player. On the other side of the shop, racks and racks of neatly arranged costumes for every occasion caused them to stop and stare at the varied hues. The shopkeeper led them to a separate room that displayed many masks to choose from, along with other accessories.

"I ordered mainly black and white masks, some with gold or silver highlights. Of course, there are solid gold and silver ones, too. Brenda told me the theme in plenty of time, so I'm prepared."

The women walked around and picked up several to try on. Emily told them to make sure they chose a mask that was a good disguise. "There will be an auction of men and women for the last dance."

"What does that mean?" Maddie asked. Emily explained that a few women and men still in their disguises would volunteer to be auctioned off for the last dance. "It's like a final, extra part of the fundraiser. It's extra fun because no one will know who they are bidding on, and won't find out until unmasking time."

Susan chose a mask after trying on four that appealed to her. She looked at the price tag and promptly put it back on the stand. Maddie drifted a few feet from her and finally declared that she had found the right one. She, too, looked at the price tag and then put it down. She asked the owner if there were others to choose from.

"I have a few that are priced lower," he said, seeing the problem. "Follow me and I'll show you." He showed them a few to the side that were rather plain and rough, and the two women started looking through them. Emily had watched the entire process. She called the owner over for a private conversation, as the two sisters browsed the array. They quickly made an agreement.

The owner turned back to Maddie and Susan. "I'm so sorry, I forgot to tell you that some of these masks are discounted for the gala since you are guests of the bed and breakfast. Let's go back and see if the ones you liked are in that category."

As it turned out, Maddie and Susan were able to afford the ones they wanted. They paid and walked around while Emily paid for hers. She discreetly handed the owner the extra money needed to cover the masks the two sisters had bought, plus enough for hers and for Jack's. She joined the two sisters, who stood outside the shop gazing upward at the deep blue sky.

"I hear there's a coffee shop down the street. Let's go get a drink. It's called Morning Sun." They walked down the sidewalk together and Emily smiled broadly as she pushed the door open for her new friends.

"I overheard Phyllis telling someone that the owner is her daughter," Susan said. "It seems all the people around here are very good friends or related to one another in some way."

At the coffee shop, they were greeted by a crowd of arriving tourists. They recognized other guests from Sheffield Bed and Breakfast and joined them for lattes.

Maddie and Susan were caught up in the spirit of expectation of the night ahead of them. Neither voiced the fact they would be mingling with a class of people that only something magical could make possible in their lives.

CHAPTER THREE

MASQUERADE GALA

B renda walked through the rooms where the party would be held, checking things one last time. Tall vases sprayed with silver and gold held long-stemmed floral arrangements, all white. Jenny proved a genius as usual, adding colored blossoms in the three gem colors that fit the theme. In the sunroom, tables with white tablecloths and black runners were set up as if in a casino. Poker chips and decks of cards were centered on each.

Brenda felt a familiar hand on her shoulder. "Everything is perfect. Let's get dressed for the big night," Mac said, with a warm, reassuring smile. Without Mac, Brenda knew her nerves would be all over the place. He was the calm she needed.

William Pendleton came through from the foyer.

"I told Phyllis I'd meet her in her apartment to get dressed and ready," he said. "I just saw Matthew Thomason outside taking a walk. He barely recognized me, but of course, it's been quite a while since we met. He appreciated the invitation for the weekend." With a wave, he went on his way to find his wife.

Brenda and Mac started for the stairs, just as Matthew Thomason walked in and greeted them. They chatted briefly and then headed for their rooms to get ready.

Brenda pulled the delicate black lace dress from the hanger. It lacked a tag like the others, but Phyllis told her it was worn by a leading actress in Randolph's last performance on stage. It slid perfectly over her body with a sleek fit. She had chosen a gold brocade Parisian mask because of the flaring feathers that reached above her forehead. Then she slipped on black wedge shoes and looked at Mac. He finished straightening his black tie and picked up the matching Venetian mask and put it on.

He took the gold herringbone necklace from her hands and clasped it behind her neck.

"Will you recognize me when you get ready to bid for our last dance together?" he teased.

"How do you know I won't bid on another handsome man?" They bantered back and forth regarding who they might choose for their final dance partners as Brenda neatened her hair and finished her makeup in the mirror.

Brenda laughed and finally turned to look at him. "Don't worry," she said, "I'd recognize those lips anywhere. I won't go wrong."

Mac swept her close and kissed her lightly. They met Emily and Jack in the hallway. The young couple looked stunning and Brenda complimented them. Mac agreed.

"I'm going to stop at Maddie and Susan's room to see if they need any help," Emily said. She turned to her husband. "Wait for me in the foyer. I'll be down soon."

At the bottom of the stairs, they were met by the employees. Brenda marveled at the variety of designs chosen. Jenny and Bryce walked through the door just then. They were dressed as two characters from Phantom of the Opera. Bryce's mask was a crooked, Phantom-style half mask, solid black. Jenny wore a full mask with silver netting that spread into an irregular shape off the right side. Her dress was solid white and she wore a simple ruby and diamond bracelet.

"Those jugglers out there are really good. That's a great way to greet everyone," Jenny said.

"It was my father's idea. He met them somewhere on his recent travels in Europe." Brenda explained why they were in town this weekend.

By this time more guests had arrived. Maddie, Susan and Emily joined them, everyone dressed in their finest and looking excited behind their fancy masquerade masks.

Everyone moved into the main area. The party was in full swing when Matthew Thomason arrived. Stationed at the entrance, Brenda recognized him behind his mask by his stooped shoulders and uncertain gait. She asked him if he played cards or poker. When he said he did, she directed him to the sunroom turned casino. At first he appeared uncertain. Mac stepped forward.

"I play some poker," he said. "I'll take you in and we'll find a table. You may know some of the guests in there, though they may be hard to recognize."

Again, Matthew hesitated. "Well, I suppose I should go in," he said, clearing his throat nervously. "The gala is the whole reason I'm here, after all." Mac smiled, wondering what had made the guest so nervous. Surely he did not feel put out by the costs—as a guest at the bed and breakfast, he didn't have to pay for a ticket to the party. Mac was under the impression that this friend of William Pendleton's was here because he had the money to be generous, but the detective found himself wondering if he no longer held the wealth he once enjoyed.

Squaring his stooped shoulders, the older man stepped toward the poker tables as if he meant to take back his rightful position. Mac noticed that Matthew's tuxedo was a little faded, but still quite impressive. Perhaps the man was simply not very social.

As it turned out, only two empty chairs were left at the tables. Mac took the one next to the table where

Matthew sat down. Matthew greeted the other three people and they decided to play poker. As Mac watched, he could see the man's confidence rising as they played the card game. Evidently he was somewhat better than the others at poker, and had realized the other three were amateurs. More than playing, he became interested in the conversation. One man stated he was expanding his technology business across the world. They talked of gains and successes. Matthew nodded as if storing their names in his mind for later use. Amused but relieved to see that the nervous guest was settling in, Mac turned to focus on his own hand of poker.

Servers circled the rooms with trays of small canapés, both savory and sweet, that the players enjoyed. Mac indulged in the parmesan-infused fries from the small bowls set in front of each player. Drinks were served and players became jocular and high spirited at a few of the tables. Mac glanced around the room and noted it was all in good fun. He was especially glad to see Matthew relax. He obviously knew how to play poker.

Brenda danced with different partners while Mac played cards. Some she recognized and others she wasn't so sure who they were. After the third whirl on the dance floor, she told Jack McAuliffe, her latest partner, that she was going to take a break and check on the food. He left her and pulled his wife Emily in for the next spin across the floor. Brenda glanced back. They made the perfect couple and definitely know how to dance with style, she thought.

As she passed the long table, she was pleased to see the smoked salmon blinis had the right amount of crème fraiche and chives. Allie and someone Brenda didn't recognize took bites of tiny pastry-wrapped bites of beef and arugula. The chef had created the sesame soy dressing that afternoon and Brenda wholeheartedly approved. Brenda moved into the sitting room where two long tables lined one wall. Numerous auction items donated by the downtown shops were placed for guests to peruse before the silent auction. She returned to the dining room and started to go into the kitchen to compliment Chef Morgan and her helpers.

The kitchen was empty except for clean drink glasses and vacant replenishing trays. The chef came back through the door.

"They're sure eating up the food," she said. "I'm glad it's going over so well."

"You are expert at this food thing," Brenda told her. "I didn't have any worries at all. Do you need any help in here?"

"Of course not. You should be out there having a good time, Brenda. We can handle this. Right now we're out in the dining area making room for more trays. Everything is under control here."

Brenda did want to return to the gala but it was her habit to pitch in, showing her employees she could be counted on for help when more hands were needed. It seemed her chef had things under control. Both women turned when the back door opened and someone came in carrying flat boxes. Brenda did not recognize the man bringing the delivery from Sweet Treats. He introduced himself as Cary Buckley. Cary was in full attire, wearing a black suit and dress shoes. He explained he had a mask and would put it on when he got everything inside.

"I told Hope I would help get these desserts over here. She'll be on her way as soon as she and David get dressed for the party. Everything is fresh and ready for you."

Brenda thanked him and the chef helped him place the boxes in the walk-in refrigerator. He went back outside to bring in more. When he returned he carried in the chocolate fountain.

"I was told to set it wherever you want it. Hope will put the fruits and stuff around it when she gets here." He glanced at his watch. "That should be any minute now."

Just as he finished his words, Hope and David came through the back door. "I have everything that goes with the fountain, Brenda. Where do you want it all? I see you've met Cary. Good." Hope was dressed for the gala, but was currently fully invested in the role of businesswoman and proud owner of Sweet Treats.

David placed a container on the counter with the cut fruit and other treats that went with the fountain. "As soon as you are finished here, come on out and have a dance with me, Hope," he said.

She paused and then smiled. "That's right. We're here to have fun, too."

Brenda directed Hope to the spot for the fountain on the smaller buffet. Her chef and two helpers followed with one box of assorted desserts and set them at the opposite end. A third kitchen assistant stayed in the kitchen to fill a smaller tray with chocolate squares to take to the game room. Another did the same with petit fours.

When they walked out, guests gathered around the chocolate fountain and admired it over and over. David pulled Hope away after she thanked them all, and swung her onto the dance floor.

Once the fountain was set up, Cary asked the chef if she wanted him to take drinks into the game room. By this time, he had his mask on and looked like an ordinary guest, not a delivery man. The chef was happy to have a pair of extra hands. She appointed one of her helpers to show him where to set things up.

After the first dance, Brenda pulled Hope aside. "Where did you find Cary?"

"He's in town getting ready to set up a real estate office. He came in for a treat and my delivery guy had just left due to a family emergency. I had no one to get things over here. He overheard me and my staff talking about the dilemma and offered to help out. He walked in just in the nick of time."

"That makes sense. I wondered why someone his age would be a delivery person. I mean, he looks like someone capable of a lot of things."

"He's thirty-eight and just helping me out in a pinch. I think he'll do well in real estate around here. He has the right personality."

Mac played one last hand before he folded and made his apologies to the other players, exiting the game room. He searched for Brenda. When he found her, he said, "Let's dance. I'm in there losing at cards." He pulled her onto the dance floor. For the hundredth time, Brenda wondered how she had lived into her forties before being held like Detective Mac Rivers held her.

"We can't have a loser around here," she said. "Is everyone else in there having a good time?"

"Yes, they seem to be. Even Matthew Thomason has loosened up. He was at the table next to me and I'd say his luck at poker is running quite well. This night should bring in a lot of money, Brenda. There's no doubt in my mind they'll want you to do this every year from here on out."

He pulled her close and they swirled around the floor. "I

have to say Bryce came through on his promise of good music," Brenda said.

"Yes, thank God," Mac said. They laughed and twirled some more.

At the end of the dance, Brenda suggested Mac go back and play cards again. She told him she had a feeling he would win now that his blood was circulating again. He took her hand and together they went into the casino room. They made their way around the room greeting everyone until Mac returned to his table and resumed playing. He wondered who the tall, capable man serving drinks might be, but Brenda left the room before he had a chance to ask her. He made a mental note to follow up later.

Brenda's curiosity about Cary—the delivery man turned server—grew as she stopped for a drink of punch, surveying the gala in full swing. She had not heard anyone around town mention anything about a new real estate office ready to open. That in itself was strange, since gossip sometimes made its way around Sweetfern Harbor even before thoughts had changed to actions. Jenny always knew everything that was going on and she hadn't said anything about it at all. Molly's Morning Sun Coffee was always the hub of gossip, but Brenda didn't recall any news about Cary Buckley or a real estate office being discussed there either.

She picked up a savory canapé and took a bite. Her mind

36

had been so consumed with the details of the evening, happily the taste brought her back to the masquerade gala in progress around her. Everywhere she looked there were twinkling lights, sumptuous costumes, and laughing guests immersed in conversation. She smiled. It was time to place her silent bid in the sitting room. Brenda had her eye on the bedside Tiffany lamp.

CHAPTER FOUR

SUDDEN INTERRUPTION

*a*t the poker tables, there was a hum of anticipation as a few guests gathered to watch the winning players. Everyone wanted to see who would win. Mac was enjoying the atmosphere of the casino room and décor, even if he wasn't winning all the time. As he looked over his cards, he was startled to hear an urgent voice across the room, rising over the conversational noise.

"Hey, pal, what's wrong?"

Mac jerked his head toward the table next to him, where Matthew Thomason had slumped over, scattering his poker chips across the floor. The detective leapt to his feet, felt for a pulse and found none. Cary set down the dessert tray in his hand and rushed to the scene. He looked at Mac, who shook his head. The detective ordered everyone to remain in the room while Cary closed the French doors that were partway open, separating the players from the revelry that continued in the rest of the bed and breakfast. Mac was on his mobile phone instantly, alerting dispatch and the police chief. Then he called Bryce and told him to come alone to the casino room. In a split second, the young detective arrived to find the card and poker players murmuring in alarm, their cards now unused on the tables.

"Paramedics are on the way, though I've called the coroner as well," Mac told Bryce. "They will come through this outside door directly into this room. Go out and tell Brenda to keep the party going as if nothing has happened. Perhaps we can avoid disturbing the big gala that way."

"Does she even know what happened?" Bryce asked.

"Not until you tell her first, and in private, Detective."

The two men and the one woman who had been playing with Matthew did not move. Mac asked them if he had shown any symptoms of illness or discomfort before he collapsed. All three stated he appeared to be having a good time. "He'd been drinking more than the rest of us," a woman named Janet said, "but he seemed fine, and we didn't see anything odd about it." She waved her hands toward the partiers. "He wasn't drinking any more than some of the others here are doing."

"He wasn't drunk, Janet." The voice came from a young man next to Janet. His black suit was cut from the finest fabric, Mac noted. The mask hid some of his facial features, but the detective still picked up that he was a handsome man.

"I didn't say he was drunk. I just said he drank more than the three of us." The other man had nothing to add.

Bryce returned to the room and pulled Mac aside. "You'd better update Brenda as soon as you can. She's a little distressed to say the least."

"I will, but knowing her, she will be just fine until I can get out there. You start taking statements on that side of the room and I'll take this side." Mac was anxious to begin with the servers, who had remained in the room as directed, as well as the three poker players at Matthew's table. He led the servers over to a quieter corner of the room.

"Did any of you see anything unusual about Mr. Thomason's actions or mannerisms?"

One server was a full-time employee of the bed and breakfast and had seen the man before the party, as well. "He wasn't as friendly as most guests are, but nothing struck me as unusual about that," she said. The server next to her shook her head without any words. Her olive skin paled and Mac noted her hands shook. He asked for her name and told her to go to the kitchen and regain her composure. "Don't talk about this to anyone, even your co-workers. This is a police investigation now, and until we know more you need to keep your statements confidential. If you don't feel able to make a statement right this moment, you can come down to the station and see me privately in the morning." The girl nodded her head and hurried to the kitchen.

Luckily, the ambulance arrived with no siren, and Mac doubted the guests noticed the flashing lights from inside the party. The paramedics briefly attempted to resuscitate the man, but he clearly had no pulse, and the quickly confirmed there was nothing else they could do for him. The coroner arrived and he and Mac began pushing several tables back from the scene. Bryce continued his way around the room, gathering any information that might help them figure out if the death was natural or foul play.

Since the scene had to be documented and the coroner had to process the body for evidence in place, the detective decided he could be spared for a short while. Mac told the coroner he would be right back. He found his wife at the table looking at nearly empty trays of food. He took her arm and pulled her into the hallway.

"Let's go into your office for privacy," he said.

William saw them hurry out and followed them. He asked if there was a problem and Mac told him something had happened to his friend Matthew Thomason in the game room.

"I thought he looked rather ill when I saw him. Of course, it's been a few years since we met and it was brief. Is he all right?"

Mac weighed his options, and realized he would need help from William to find and contact the next of kin. He sighed and looked at William, and then at Brenda. "He's dead," Mac said. He ushered William and Brenda into the office where he explained what had happened.

"I can only assume he had a heart attack or something like that," Brenda said, aghast. But her brow creased in doubt even as she said it, and she hadn't missed the tension in Mac's jawline and shoulders, either. Deep in her gut, Brenda feared it was no accident.

Brenda felt William's eyes scrutinizing her. She sensed he may be holding something back about the wealthy guest who had just dropped dead in the middle of one the biggest, most important nights ever hosted at the Sheffield Bed and Breakfast. She held her thoughts for now. William seemed in shock, though he quietly offered to fetch his address book so he could provide the detective with the contact information he had for William's family.

Mac returned to the game room. Bryce had taken statements from the other guests, and all had willingly provided contact information. Cary Buckley asked if it was all right to gather empty glasses and other utensils from the tables.

"Don't take anything from the table where Mr. Thomason played, or from the tables surrounding his." Mac watched the man gather plates and glasses from the far tables and then turn to the door to carry them to the kitchen. "Tell the chef not to wash anything until further notice, please." Mr. Buckley nodded somberly and headed for the kitchen to notify the chef, who had been given the same instructions by Brenda.

Brenda saw Cary when he returned to the dining room buffet to continue pouring drinks for guests who still had no clue of what had just happened.

Tim Sheffield approached his daughter. "Brenda, I know something's going on. What is it?"

The light had gone from her eyes. "A man just dropped dead in the game room, Dad. Mac isn't sure if it was natural causes or foul play. I'm hoping it was something like a heart attack. I can't believe it happened on such a wonderful night. Everything was going so well."

Tim nodded, understanding that most guests had no idea what had just occurred, since the party continued in full swing around them. Auction items were being sold and money flowed like fast-moving water. Despite the somber events in one room, the gaiety and celebration continued in the other rooms. "I'm sure he died of natural causes,

Brenda. Maybe he was under a lot of stress and it became too much for him. Just leave it to the coroner to figure it all out, and try to enjoy the rest of the night." He smiled at her. "It's almost midnight and time for the mask unveiling. Did you bid on Mac for the last dance?"

"I haven't placed any bids at all for the last dance and I'm sure Mac will be tied up in the middle of the investigation, anyway."

"Well, if you don't have a partner, you always have your dad."

Brenda gave Tim a quick hug. Most of the casino room players had exited through the sunroom door and blended into the throngs of party-goers by then. Brenda sensed that whispers had already started, though the news hadn't reached the majority of the guests yet. It was only a matter of time. Sweetfern Harbor was a hotbed of gossip and she only hoped the success of the fundraiser would not be overshadowed by rumors and innuendoes about the death of Matthew Thomason.

"Did something just happen in the poker room, Brenda?" Hope Williams tugged at her arm with a strange look on her face. "I heard someone say the paramedics were here. David said he saw the coroner's van outside, too. Did— did someone actually die in there?" Her voice dropped to a scandalized hush.

Brenda breathed deeply. "Mac wants to keep it under

wraps as much as possible for now. We can't have the guests panicking and the crime scene compromised. They're still investigating. Please don't pass anything around this early." She told her friend as much as she could, and both agreed it must have been a natural death. Brenda saw Cary reach for a savory canapé and pop it in his mouth. She decided to change the topic of conversation. "Tell me again about this Cary Buckley, Hope. Where did he come from?"

"I'm not sure exactly, but someplace in Massachusetts, I believe. He showed me his real estate license. He seemed proud of it. I think he'll be an asset around here, as I told you." She stood back. "Why are you so curious about him?"

Brenda shrugged her shoulders. "It just strikes me as odd —isn't it funny that this town is so full of gossip but I never heard anything about him until today? But I suppose everyone thought I was a stranger when I first arrived here, too."

"No one thought badly of you, Brenda. Everyone missed Randolph, of course, he was so much a part of our town. We were just curious about you, same as you are about Cary. As for you, back then you had a lot to learn about how we are all one big family around here." Her eyes sparkled with the teasing, and Brenda had to agree.

After hearing the news of Matthew Thomason's sudden death, William Pendleton got to work. He called his personal assistant, who was still at the mansion working late on some business plans, and asked her to look up any addresses associated with Mr. Thomason from his old address book. After they hung up, he became curious about the man. He went into the empty hallway and pulled out his cell phone. He began his search and found a trove of articles about the recent happenings with Matthew's textile business. After ten minutes had passed he turned the phone off and put it in his pocket. At last he understood the emaciated and strained look Matthew Thomason wore before his death.

William rubbed a hand over his face as he rejoined the party, distracted by what he had read. The articles had delved into the boom and spectacular bust of a textile business venture. He idly wondered what had happened to Matthew's business partner, Arthur Blodgett, when everything fell apart. The financial losses seemed enormous, perhaps enough to wreck Matthew and damage his health. Had this partner, Arthur, been able to recoup his share of the losses in some way? He took out his phone again and intrigued, began reading some more.

Brenda and Hope were chatting about the silent auction items in the sitting room when Phyllis joined them. "Have you seen William?" she asked.

"I think I saw him go out into the hall a bit ago," Hope said.

"Again?" Phyllis said. "He's been on that phone for at

least forty-five minutes. I hoped he would join me and have some fun. The whole point was for us to mingle with the guests he invited. What's going on with him?" Her eyes landed on Brenda, who looked away uneasily. "Oh boy. Brenda, I know that look. What's going on?"

Brenda told her the events in a hushed tone. "William may be trying to do some research on Matthew. I don't know that for sure, but he did tell me they had met several years ago and that he had looked much healthier than he did when he got here."

"Come on, ladies. Let's forget all of this for now," Hope said. "It's almost time to unveil the masks and I want to make sure no one bids higher on David than I have. I'd like to finish the night in the arms of my husband out on the dance floor."

The distraction was a welcome relief. Brenda knew there was work yet to come on the matter of Matthew. The three women headed for the dance floor where the final auction totals were announced, then, after a drumroll, everyone began taking their masks off. Brenda saw that Mac was nowhere in sight. Tim took his daughter's arm and led her to the dance floor once the auctioned men and women were revealed. It felt good to have her father's protective arms around her.

Mac came to the doorway of the room and nodded his appreciation to Tim. He returned to the sunroom to oversee the careful collection of evidence. Then, as it turned out, everyone was having such a good time that Brenda told the band to keep playing a couple more dance numbers. She searched for William and found him in the dining room, still thumbing through his phone.

"It doesn't look good after I looked into Matthew's background," William said, slipping his phone back into his pocket. "He lost everything he owned and was sued by some of his creditors. One article I read said that when his business declared bankruptcy, he listed himself as penniless, except for one bank account with a minimal amount of funds."

Mac and Bryce stepped into the room. Just then Jenny entered and chided Bryce for ducking out on the last dance with her. He explained what had happened in a tense undertone. Her face went pale and she had no words.

Mac looked at Brenda. "The coroner just called me. He said Matthew was poisoned, most likely tonight. He doesn't have the full report yet, of course, but based on early blood test results, he is certain the man didn't die of natural causes."

Brenda looked at the almost-empty food trays. She folded her arms and clutched her elbows. "Do you think my food had anything to do with it?"

Mac assured her that couldn't be the case, since Matthew was the only one affected. "No one else seems ill, much less ready to keel over." He looked at the buffet. "But, we still have to test everything, to be safe and thorough. Don't let your workers or chef clean anything yet. Bryce, get some of the officers in here taking samples of every morsel and every opened liquor bottle."

"Maybe someone spiked one of his drinks, or served him food poisoned just for him," Brenda said.

Mac nodded. "That's my take on it for now. It will take the lab quite a while to get through all the testing they'll have to do. We'll be waiting on a lot of lab results." Mac and Bryce headed for the police station to start processing witness statements. Mac gave Brenda a quick kiss on the cheek to reassure her before he left.

As a group of plainclothes police officers swarmed over the kitchens and tables to collect samples, the band finished playing the last dance piece with a flourish, and everyone began to gather their belongings. They thanked Brenda for the night of fun and many expressed the desire to do it again the following year. The accountant from the hospital gushed that she was certain they'd raised the largest amount in a one-night fundraiser that the hospital had ever experienced. Brenda thanked everyone for coming and stayed at the door bidding each guest farewell. Once they were gone, she then turned to face the fact that the night was far from over. She and Phyllis went into the kitchen. Two officers were finishing up and told Brenda they could clean up at any time in there. Phyllis and Brenda looked at one another and laughed out loud.

"Let's get to it. I don't want Chef Anna to come in tomorrow morning to this mess," Brenda said, taking an apron down from a hook on the wall and handing another to Phyllis. She had already dismissed all the other workers since there was nothing more they could do. Bryce had taken their names and contact information. Brenda and Phyllis worked for two hours, wrapping leftovers and washing dishes as Jenny carried them in from the dining room, once they had been sampled for evidence and testing. When she had carried in the last plate, Jenny quietly took down another apron and grabbed a dish towel to help the two women in the kitchen as they cleaned up after the magnificent gala, and unexpectedly tragic night.

CHAPTER FIVE

SOMETHING FAMILIAR

*L*ater that night, Brenda climbed the stairs to her second floor apartment. The upstairs hall was quiet and most of the guest rooms were dark, but she saw that Maddie and Susan's door stood open a little, spilling a bit of light into the hallway. She wondered if she should ask if they had heard any rumors, but something made her hesitate. Instead, she lingered at her apartment door for a moment and listened to their animated chatter as they wound down from the party.

Maddie flopped on the pillow-top bed and sighed audibly. "Wasn't that the most wonderful night you've ever had, Susan? I felt like I was in a fairytale that ended perfectly."

"It really was the best time of my life. I had fun for the

first time in a long while. Thank you, Maddie, for inviting me to share this weekend getaway that you won."

From where she stood, Brenda could hear the sound of Susan's necklace as she removed it. Susan had worn a necklace with an ornate gold chain and an emerald-green pendant that night. "I can't tell if this is real or not."

Maddie laughed. "Allie said that it's costume jewelry, but neither of us has ever owned real jewelry, so how would we know?" There was a pause and Brenda heard the rustle of the bedcovers being pulled down. "By the way, did you see that waiter, Cary Buckley?"

"The one serving drinks? I heard his name several times but I didn't meet him face to face. Why do you ask?"

"He just seemed very familiar. He asked me to dance once and when I looked in his eyes I thought I recognized him from somewhere, even behind the mask. I forgot to pay attention when everyone took their masks off later."

"I saw him unmasked," Susan said. "I guess now that you mention it, maybe there was something a little familiar about him, but I have no idea what it was."

"When he danced with me I felt like he was holding me prisoner or something. It was a feeling of control, somehow." She sighed. "Anyway, he can't spoil my night," Maddie said, and finally closed the door.

As Sheffield Bed and Breakfast grew quiet, Brenda had a lot to think about.

Once Brenda sat down in her apartment and opened her computer, she searched for Cary Buckley. It was just as Hope had told her. He acquired his real estate license two years ago and joined a real estate firm in Boston. On his professional website, he had an announcement section where he had posted a notice, saying he had decided to relocate to Sweetfern Harbor and establish his own business. No details were given regarding his new address, but Brenda figured he just hadn't had time to update his website. She kept searching to find out about his earlier life. There were a few articles from when he won a young professional award early in his career. His father was not mentioned. It seemed he grew up with his sister, in the home of his mother.

Brenda searched on his mother's name next. It was a rags to riches story. She began as a single mother, financially strapped, but determined to make something of herself. She got her Certified Nursing Assistant license, and continued her education, moving up in the field to become a Registered Nurse before remarrying. There were articles congratulating her on her accomplishment since she had done this while working nights and weekends to support her family. Brenda read that she was currently the Director of Nursing at a well-known Boston hospital. Cary's sister, Amanda, had married a Frenchman and now lived in Paris.

Brenda's eyes fluttered. She was exhausted. If she planned to help solve the case of Matthew Thomason's poisoning she would have to be on full alert. She closed her computer with the intention of resuming her research the next day.

"Looks like tomorrow is already here," she said aloud, gazing at the pale blue light just visible through the curtains. With barely enough energy to remove her clothes, she finally sank into her bed and fell asleep.

At the police station, Mac and Bryce put on fresh coffee. "If you want to go on home, Bryce, go ahead. We'll have plenty waiting for us here in the morning."

"It is morning, boss," Bryce said. The clock on the wall next to Mac's desk read three a.m.

"In that case, why don't we both get some sleep? We'll make a fresh pot when we come back. Let the desk sergeant know this is here and the night shift will drink this in no time."

The two men parted ways in the parking lot and headed home. When Mac quietly rolled onto his side of the bed, he realized nothing was going to awaken his wife. His eyes closed and he too was in a deep sleep in no time at all.

Brenda rarely set an alarm clock. No matter what time she went to bed, for some reason she usually awoke at seven every morning. She sat up in bed and noted Mac still slept soundly. She decided to put coffee on and warm up a cinnamon roll in their apartment before she woke him up. At seven-thirty he rolled over to the aroma of coffee brewing. He jumped into the shower, dressed and joined Brenda in their small eat-in kitchen.

"I see you're getting an early start with breakfast up here," he said. He bent over and kissed her. She pushed the steaming coffee his way and agreed she needed some time away from guests for a while.

"Last night was enough company around here to last me a lifetime," she said, suppressing a yawn.

"At least you won't have any crowds this morning." They drank their beverages in mutual silence. "I'll take a cinnamon roll, if you have another one up here."

"I have some stashed for emergencies," Brenda said. She heated one up for him. "Did you find out anything new last night?"

"I had Bryce look into Matthew's background. Of course, he found exactly what William told us, for the most part. We finally packed it in around three, figuring we'd pick it up again today with fresh eyes. Bryce said he wanted to look into Matthew's business partner to see if anyone here last night may have had connections with him."

"That's a good start. I researched Cary Buckley last night and wanted to keep going but I couldn't keep my eyes open. That's where I'm starting today."

Mac raised his eyebrows. "Why do you think he has anything to do with it?"

"I'm not so sure he does. There is just something about him that seems a little mysterious to me, and I'm not the only one who thinks so. I overheard a few guests mention him as well. Don't ask me why at this point, because I don't know. It's just a feeling I have. It will probably amount to nothing."

Mac learned long before marrying Brenda Sheffield that her intuition was stronger than any evidence. It has been proven time and time again, so he didn't question her now. "I think I'll have the chef make me a quick egg sandwich and be on my way. Let me know if you find out anything at all and I'll keep you posted. Bob asked me first thing if you were in on this investigation. I assured him you were."

Chief Bob Ingram admired the astute insights Brenda Rivers had when it came to solving crimes. He had actually hoped she would become a full-fledged detective, but she declined. He did eventually convince her to accept an honorary detective position. She agreed mainly because of her love for solving crimes.

After Mac left, Brenda realized that among her guests at the masquerade gala last night was a murderer. It was not a good feeling.

She went downstairs and greeted her bed and breakfast guests. All were talking about the party the night before. By now, everyone knew that Matthew Thomason had died at the poker table. Brenda knew they wanted answers and spoke up over the breakfast table. All eyes turned to her.

"I know you are aware of the death of a guest. As it stands right now, it is believed he may have died from natural causes." She felt the need to go with her own first impression. "The police are working hard to investigate, along with the coroner. I hope this won't spoil your visit here."

All assured her it would not. Right now, Brenda had no intention of telling them the man was murdered. She tried not to drum her fingers impatiently as she waited out the breakfast conversations. Brenda wanted her guests to feel reassured by her presence. She wanted to get back to her computer research soon, but first she wanted to thank her chef again for the hard work.

"Rumor has it that Matthew Thomason was murdered last night," Chef Morgan said to Brenda.

"How did that get out?"

"You know how this town is. I asked your father about it when we were instructed to leave the dishes for the plainclothes officers to inspect. He played dumb at first, but I could tell the rumor was true." She looked closely at Brenda. "How did it happen?"

"It is true, but please don't add to the gossip. It's a police investigation and they are questioning everyone. Actually, they think he was poisoned. They were thorough in gathering evidence last night and they'll probably be back to ask questions again of everyone here. That includes employees and guests alike. They'll probably search your cabinets, too."

"I went to bed wondering if my food had anything to do with it," Morgan said with a sigh.

"No, Anna, it didn't. No one else had any ill effects at all."

Relief spread across the chef's face. "I'm sure with Mac and Chief Ingram on it, they'll find out what happened." Brenda agreed with her.

Phyllis and Allie were chatting at the front desk about the events of the night before. It seems Allie had all the information about the death of Matthew Thomason. The town was buzzing, Brenda realized. She told them if needed her, they could find her in her office. Neither of the women asked any questions.

They knew how to read Brenda, and now was not the time.

Obligations complete, Brenda opened her laptop and picked up her search about Cary Buckley. She skimmed past another article about how his mother had worked hard to arrive at her present position. She found a marriage announcement for his sister, who had made a successful marriage with someone named Pierre Bossart, a native of France she met in law school. They settled in Paris, where they remained today.

She continued researching topics about Cary Buckley. She almost scrolled past an important tidbit buried in an interview with his mother. Cary had not always been Cary Buckley. Brenda wondered about his original surname, but it was not mentioned. He had changed his last name when his mother remarried while he was still in his teens. All the articles about him and his family were dated after his mother's second marriage. Brenda was distracted by a commotion and realized she was hearing the raised voices of Maddie and Susan. The name Cary Buckley reached her ears and she closed the laptop to join them. She would not pass up the opportunity to ask them what they knew about this man.

"Come into the sitting room for a chat, if you have time," she said to them.

The sisters glanced at one another and Susan spoke first. "We wanted to tell you how wonderful the gala was last night anyway. We were so lucky to be here this weekend."

"I'm so glad you enjoyed it. I noticed you both didn't lack for dance partners." She invited them to sit and join her. "I overheard you mention Cary Buckley's name. Do you know him?"

"Actually, we've been trying to remember how we knew him since last night after the party," Maddie said. "It finally hit us. He has changed quite a bit, but he has grown up, so that is understandable" Brenda waited, wondering if this was something more than a simple coincidence. "We finally remembered he was from our neighborhood when we were growing up. We knew his sister Amanda, too. I heard she married a rich man from Paris. It's so romantic."

"What was he like growing up?"

"He was all right," Susan said with a shrug. "He is closer to Maddie's age than mine, so she was around him and Amanda a lot more than I was." She turned to her sister.

"He is actually a few years younger than I am. I'm thirty-four, so he must be thirty-one or so. He played with all the neighborhood kids like all of us did. There was always something different about him, though. Even as a kid he never seemed all that happy." She sat forward. "And by the way, his last name wasn't Buckley back then. He was younger when we knew him, so it was before his mother remarried. His last name was Thomason. We thought that was quite a coincidence when we heard that the man who died was named Matthew Thomason. Maybe that's what triggered my thinking last night."

Brenda bolted forward. "Are you sure his last name was Thomason?" Both sisters nodded their heads. "What was his father's name?"

"He didn't have a father in the home. He and Amanda were raised by his mother. I guess that's why he never seemed all that happy," Maddie said. "He probably missed having a father. They were poor, too."

"No one in our neighborhood grew up rich," Susan added, "but their family was really poor. His mother struggled. We never knew his father, so he must have left or divorced Cary's mother when the children were quite young." She paused. "It's funny that Cary once had the same last name as Matthew. What a coincidence."

"Thanks for talking with me. If you're headed downtown you'll find some interesting shops. I hope you enjoy your day." Brenda stood up, anxious to go.

"We will. Emily is going with us to browse through the shops. We will cherish the memories of last night every time we look at the masks we bought," Susan said. "We can make sure the costumes are cleaned if you'll tell us where we should take them."

"Phyllis will take care of getting them cleaned. There is a

dry cleaner downtown that specializes in cleaning vintage fabrics for us."

Brenda hurried back to her computer, hoping she wasn't rude to her guests by rushing away. At her office door she looked back and was relieved to see that Emily had joined the sisters.

Returning to her research, she next typed in the name Cary Thomason. The sisters had been right. Until his mother remarried, he retained that last name, which must have been the name of his mother's first husband. When his step-father adopted the siblings, Cary and Amanda both took his last name, Buckley, a name he still used. Brenda called Mac right away to tell him her discoveries.

"Sounds like you may have been right to suspect something wasn't quite right about Cary Buckley, Brenda. Your instincts always open up new avenues to these cases. Thank you." Mac paused a second. "Do you want to meet me for lunch downtown?"

"I'd like that," Brenda said. "We don't spend enough time like that together. Do you want to meet me at Morning Sun Coffee? I haven't had one of Molly's sandwiches in a while, plus I could call to have her save us a table in the back corner."

Mac laughed. "So much for a lunch date. With a private table we always end up discussing a case, no matter how hard we try not to."

64

As soon as she hung up, she glanced at her watch. She had another hour before lunch with Mac. She had already gotten the name of Matthew's partner from William. She needed to know more about him and returned to her research with renewed energy. She learned, as expected, that Arthur Blodgett had an impressive background in business and finance. He set up partnerships in foreign countries as a young man and easily cultivated relationships with individuals who helped spur his ventures forward. He met Matthew Thomason when they were in college. She read in an article from the online newsletter archive from their college that Matthew Thomason married a girl he knew for a total of one month before they tied the knot. She found a treasure trove of information in an old lawsuit that had been filed against Matthew during the bankruptcy. From the beginning, Arthur had apparently realized his business partner's marriage was not a happy one, but without Mia's constant support, the textile partnership would not have made it as far as it did. Their son was born not long after the marriage, which made Brenda wonder if that had been another factor in the hasty nuptials.

Matthew was smart and knew a lot about textiles. He needed Arthur's ties to the European market. Arthur put up with the fact that Matthew was a narcissistic person because Mia balanced him out, and Matthew's business savvy led them to make some very lucrative deals.

However, the work took its toll and sometimes Matthew took unacceptable risks. Mia began to lose patience with her husband's ego-driven style, and in a desperate bid to regain his love and attention, went to the bank and gave the loan officer information about a risky deal Matthew was working on. The bank changed the terms of the largest business loan. This marked the beginning of the end.

Matthew Thomason did not take his wife's interference well. Rather than reconcile with his wife and save the business, he left her and doomed the partnership to failure. In the court filing, Brenda read a painful passage where Arthur's lawyer detailed exactly how this had ended for Matthew's family. "In addition to monetary damages detailed in Section II (see above), the Plaintiff lost complete respect for his business partner M. Thomason when said individual abandoned his wife, son and daughter. Furthermore, the defendant made no provisions for his family and they were suddenly thrown out in the cold. For this reason, the Plaintiff A. Blodgett is suing for full control of the business..."

Brenda shook her head sadly and rubbed her eyes. It was difficult to reconcile the sad, frail man she had seen as a harmless guest at her bed and breakfast with the image of this narcissistic businessman capable of leaving his family.

What Brenda could not discover through her research was that unknown to Mia, Arthur Blodgett later set up a scholarship for her to pursue her nursing education. He admired her for the way she took hold of her fate and finally arrived in a secure position.

He watched from afar the progress the two children made, waiting until Mia remarried a man who appreciated her. For many years after that he stayed distant from their family, not wanting to interfere. The next time he came face to face with Cary, he saw that the boy who had been abandoned long ago by his egotistical father had grown into a man, and Arthur saw determination for revenge in his eyes and mannerisms. He realized that by what he chose to say to Cary, he could either nudge him towards revenge, or convince the young man to make something of himself and not follow the darker path of his father. Arthur had choices to make.

CHAPTER SIX

THE DEED

*ary was nine years old when along with his sister and mother, he moved from their penthouse in New York to the small town of Stockton, Massachusetts. He looked out the car window as his mother drove deeper into one shabby neighborhood after another. The blocks seemed endless to Cary, but in reality the neighborhood they settled in was only a few blocks away from the better side of the town. Most of the houses in his new neighborhood sported chipped paint, and some had foundations with broken bricks loose on the ground. Gardens of flowers brought the only beauty to the area.

Children played in the streets until a car came along, then scurried to the curb waiting for it to pass. They stared at the family who arrived in the sleek car, and were more astonished to see it pull into the driveway of a bungalow that had been empty for the past six months. Dead leaves scattered across the sidewalk and up the steps. The children gazed in awe as they watched the family carry suitcases to the front door.

"Who lives here?" Amanda asked her mother.

Mia turned and smiled bravely. "We do. This is our new home. I'll unlock the door and both of you can go on in and explore. The two bedrooms upstairs will be yours." She glanced at her son, who stood back. Cary's sullen face told her that he would prove to be one more hurdle for her to master. "Go ahead, Cary. We can all make the best of things for a while."

"We don't even have a doorman," he complained. "Who will carry the luggage up?" His mother didn't answer him and he walked into the dim house to explore the unfamiliar surroundings.

From that day forward, young Amanda fit right in with her new friends, while Cary often stood on the sidelines. His mother sold the luxury car a week after moving to the neighborhood and came home with a small compact Chevrolet that looked like it might last a month or two. With care, Mia made sure it lasted two more years. She took odd jobs while the children were in school and joined in with other mothers in planning summer block parties. Eventually, young Cary fit in enough to avoid bullying and teasing.

Meanwhile, deep down, Cary's resentment of his father grew. It didn't take long for him to realize his rich father had left his mother to fend for herself and the children. This realization came after he had pummeled his mother with questions about new clothes for school, and why he couldn't have a bicycle like the other boys, until finally she sat down privately with him to explain the situation. She told him the day would come when they would have everything they needed again. She never said a harsh word against his father, but she never talked about him, either. In fact, she never even said his name. Cary loved his mother and silently vowed to not distress her again over the matter. When she worked late at night, he made sure Amanda had a meal and helped by cleaning the kitchen so his mother wouldn't have to.

When he was a young teenager, his mother met a man and fell in love. This was not a quick marriage like her first one. It took quite a while before Cary learned to trust Robert Buckley. By the time the man became his step-father, they had developed a good relationship. Cary readily agreed to get rid of the name Thomason when Robert asked to adopt the two children. He wanted no part of his father's legacy, including his name. His birth father had signed away his legal rights to the children without a fuss. Once again, Cary belonged to an intact family and he began to focus on his future.

In the meantime, Arthur Blodgett watched it all from a distance and was pleased to see how well Mia was doing.

Her husband Robert encouraged her to go farther in her nursing career. Arthur secretly set up college scholarships for Amanda and Cary when they attended the local university. Mia often expressed how lucky they were to have received full scholarships, not knowing that Arthur had privately made arrangements to cover their expenses. She was happy both her children could complete their higher educations. For her that was a significant milestone, given the rough second start they had made as a family after leaving their New York penthouse all those years ago.

What Arthur could not have foreseen was a new connection with his former business partner's family years later, when the academically talented Amanda Buckley entered law school. Arthur's wife Lily taught law classes at the local university. Lily Blodgett's much younger brother, Pierre Bossart, was in Lily's class, and immediately took a liking to Amanda. Lily saw the chemistry between the two gifted students and made sure they connected.

Arthur had discreetly asked both Mia and Lily to avoid giving the children any unnecessary information about the long-past partnership. For his own part, he wanted his secret generosity toward the family to remain anonymous, as well. At some point after Amanda and Pierre's marriage, however, he found himself sitting across from Cary Buckley in Boston one afternoon. Cary had requested a meeting since they both worked in the city. It was the first time Arthur had seen him in years. He noted the handsome and matured young man.

Cary told Arthur of his plans to move to Sweetfern Harbor and set up his own real estate practice. After a long discussion, Arthur Blodgett discovered the real reason his secret protégé wanted to relocate to the little coastal town. He was cagey about his exact plans, but made it clear that he knew his biological father would be in Sweetfern Harbor eventually, and that Cary planned to use the opportunity to exact a little revenge. Cary mimed someone sick to their stomach, caving over. Arthur chuckled and understood Cary's feeling toward his father, and privately thought a little stomach illness would not be detrimental to his former partner.

Arthur and Lily Blodgett procured tickets for the masquerade gala fundraiser, as Arthur was a long-time supporter of the hospital. Their costumes were exquisite and faces hidden well with their masks. Arthur was shocked to see his former partner, whose haggard appearance was barely concealed by the mask he chose.

Arthur had carried out his own form of revenge, over the years. He had taken care to beat Matthew down by weaseling him into bad deals after he had left his family penniless. Arthur Blodgett's name failed to appear on any of the transactions. He made sure of that. In the end, the narcissistic Matthew Thomason was worse off than the family he left behind. In his reduced state, Matthew was probably happy to attend the gala simply for the free food. He had no idea Arthur was there and he did not recognize his own son, even when Cary's mask was off. Cary was the last person on his mind.

Cary Buckley had never allowed his mind to waver from what he knew his birth father deserved. When he had discovered Matthew Thomason was a connection of the wealthy William Pendleton in Sweetfern Harbor, it was an easy decision to relocate his real estate business there. He knew it would only be a matter of time before Mr. Pendleton invited his business connections to an event.

It had been easy to fall into the role of volunteer bartender and fill-in server. Everyone in Sweetfern Harbor was drawn to Cary as soon as he spoke, with his easy conversation and smooth charm. Everyone except Brenda Rivers. Cary did not miss the questioning glances she sent his way. Rumors around town mentioned her involvement when it came to solving cases alongside local law enforcement. He had not banked on that, or the fact her husband was the lead detective at the local police station.

Cary was nothing if not an astute planner. He ensured that his careful plan would work.

When the chef and her helpers were in the kitchen, they chattered away about details needed to be done in the dining room and in the casino room. From the conversation, he surmised they would be out there long enough for him to prepare his next move. Once the last person was out of the kitchen, he reached into his shirt pocket for the small vial. Just as he prepared to dose the opened liquor bottle with a few drops, the back door opened.

He quickly capped the vial and shoved it into his pocket.

"That's a good vintage whiskey," William Pendleton said.

Cary turned with a broad smile on his face. "I've heard it is. Someone in the card room asked for it specifically. I'm sure we'll go through several bottles once he lets everyone know what he's enjoying. I hope it won't break the bank of the hostess."

William told him he was personally covering all the expenses so they wouldn't be deducted from the donations to the hospital. "Everyone here is having such a good time, don't worry about the cost. Our guests should have the best," he said, clapping the man on the shoulder absently as he walked away.

William left to join his wife. Cary muttered expletives and carried the bottle out to the buffet. He poured several shots and placed them on the tray the server readied for the game room. "Be sure to brag about the vintage," Cary said, with his trademark grin. The server smiled back.

He knew he must remain as if things were normal. He watched William snatch a shot from the tray as the server passed him. The server turned and told him he had chosen a good vintage whiskey.

"Yes, I have." William lifted the shot glass toward Cary as if toasting his choice.

At that moment, Cary knew he had to come up with a different plan. He edged toward the doorway and saw his father well into his game of poker. He heard him tell the server he preferred a good stout red wine. When she came through the door, Cary told her he would open a bottle of the best right away. He went down the back staircase into the wine cellar and chose an ordinary house wine. There was some satisfaction in serving his miser of a birth father a cheap glass of red for his last drink, when he thought he was going to get an expensive vintage.

When he came upstairs, he poured most of the bottle down the sink and then the remaining wine into a wine glass on the buffet. In the dim yellow lantern lights no one noticed the clear poison in the bottom of the glass. He set it on the tray along with other drinks, none of which held wine. He picked a different server and told her to take the wine to a certain table and offer the other drinks to players sitting there.

"Lindy just told me someone at that table wanted a good red wine." He pointed to his father's table. "I'm not sure who, but just ask when you get there."

The server nodded and did as told. Cary watched his father lift his finger signaling he had ordered red wine.

Cary watched out of the corner of his eye as Matthew Thomason sipped the deadly drink. Cary turned to ask a server on break if she wanted to dance. They were not far from the door leading to the game room. She munched a sweet canapé.

"I'd rather get off my feet," she said. "I think I'll go sit in the kitchen for my break. I'll have to take another one of these snacks along though."

"Try the fries, too. They are the best."

At the moment the server left him, Matthew Thomason slumped to his death while his chip winnings scattered noisily onto the tiled floor. Inwardly, Cary felt triumph surge through his body. Outwardly, he jumped into action and rushed to the table. He stood back and watched the detective feel for an absent pulse.

In the other room, Lily and Arthur Blodgett continued to dance. The band played a lively tune. When they took a rest from the dance floor, Arthur suggested they get something to eat. The tables were laden with replenished trays of food. He noticed two people hurry to the game room. He wondered if Cary had managed to sicken his father and hoped the act of petty revenge would satisfy the young man. The bitterness Cary held was deep. Arthur told Lily to go ahead and mingle without him.

"I'm going to have a stiff drink and join Roger White over there. He has a good connection I may be able to contact in Belgium."

"Can't you get away from business for one night?" Lily kissed him lightly on the cheek.

Arthur chatted with Roger only because the man was standing close to the game room. The sliding door had been closed off, but perhaps he could overhear something. He and the financier discussed business in Belgium, even though Arthur was only half paying attention. Twenty minutes passed before Detective Rivers came out into the room. He stood for a second looking over the crowd. Arthur watched as he pulled the hostess, Brenda, out of the room and into the hallway. Arthur suppressed a smirk. He presumed paramedics had been called to take poor Matthew to the hospital, no doubt using a side entrance to avoid disturbing the rest of the gala guests. The doors remained closed to the rest of the bed and breakfast. There was no sign yet of Cary.

The look on Cary Buckley's face when he sauntered from the game room caused an alarm to go off in Arthur's head. The young man's face relaxed and he beamed, but there was a dark gleam of triumph in his eyes.

"It's done, Arthur. Matthew Thomason will never throw his ego in everyone's face again. I made sure of that."

Arthur stared at him. Cary laughed softly and walked away as if nothing was going on in the next room. Arthur caught up with him and pulled him around to face him. "What did you do?"

"He ordered a good vintage red wine and I made sure he got it. Of course, I didn't fetch the best wine of the house for him. He didn't deserve an expensive last drink like that." His eyes glazed over. "I wonder what will happen to all that money he accumulated." He turned back to Arthur as if brought back to reality. "I suppose the company is all yours now, Arthur."

Arthur Blodgett recovered his voice. "He lost everything ages ago. He is penniless and we are no longer partners."

"Is that a fact?" Cary commented. "That's even more satisfying. I guess he found out what being poor really feels like." Cary meandered to the table and picked up a single serving of caviar-infused fries.

Arthur, still in shock, searched for his wife. Lily's eyes held alarm when she saw his face. "What's wrong with you, Arthur? Are you ill?"

"I don't feel well. I think this crowd is getting to me. Would you mind if I go on along home, my dear? You stay and enjoy the rest of the evening. I'll call the driver,

Edward. He will take me home and bring the limo back here for you."

Lily protested but Arthur assured her he would be fine. "I'll call home in a half-hour or so and check on you, Arthur."

He smiled and told her he looked forward to hearing her voice.

CHAPTER SEVEN

CONSCIENCE CLEARING

It was a couple days after Matthew Thomason was poisoned at the gala. Brenda felt certain Cary Buckley had something to do with it, but the first two days after the gala had been consumed with clean-up, crime scene processing, and Mac's officers following early leads and waiting for lab tests to come back. For her part, Brenda had filled an entire day just contacting all of the servers and bartenders that had been in the casino room that evening, asking for additional details.

As soon as Brenda awoke and realized she had a free morning, she knew her first order of business was to go downtown and visit Cary's new real estate office in Sweetfern Harbor.

The cool wind from the ocean soothed her senses and she took deep breaths as she stepped out the front door of the

Sheffield Bed and Breakfast, savoring the salt breeze. Spring was coming faster than usual, indicated by the early flowers attempting to push their way up through the earth.

"Brenda, I'll walk with you if you don't mind," Tim Sheffield said.

"I'm glad you showed up. I need your company, Dad."

They walked in silence. Tim waited for his daughter to speak first. He had the feeling she had a lot on her mind. She was like his wife in that neither spoke until they thought out their words. Both also had to decide who was worthy of their thoughts. He smiled at the memory of his wife, still missed by both husband and daughter.

"Dad, I'm going to see Cary Buckley. Hope told me he's opening a real estate office. In fact, he rented the office in town only a couple of days before the fundraiser." She looked at her father. "I'm sure you've heard by now that my guest Matthew Thomason was murdered."

Tim nodded. "I heard that."

"I think Cary had something to do with Matthew's murder." Brenda told Tim the details of Cary's life. "There was something about him the other night that didn't sit well with me. I have to talk to him."

"I'll come in with you to welcome him."

"I want to make this a casual visit, Dad. I'll go in alone. It'll be fine."

"Okay, if you're sure, but please be careful. I'll be at Morning Sun Coffee if you need me. I'm on your speed dial, aren't I?"

"Of course you are," Brenda said. It felt good to have a light moment before they parted ways in front of the refurbished brick building a few storefronts down from Sweet Treats. As she approached the building, she could see it had been restored and renovated into offices with windows looking out onto Main Street. She saw no sign in the window, but could see Cary clearly through the glass, so she went ahead and opened the door.

Cary stood and greeted Brenda when she entered. She glanced at the office surroundings. Two potted plants sat side by side as if waiting for a place of their own. Two new chairs and a small table were against the side wall of the room. An empty rack nailed to the wall waited to be filled with housing flyers and information for homebuyers. She didn't see any sign of phones or computers yet.

"Your masquerade gala seemed to be a huge success," Cary said. "I had a good time, even while working. Your chef generously offered us breaks in between running all over the place."

They discussed the party a bit and Brenda asked him if

he knew any of the guests. He stated that he had recognized two he knew while he lived in Boston, which he had also mentioned to Bryce in his official witness statement. Otherwise, he only knew the people he had met since arriving in Sweetfern Harbor. Brenda opted not to bring up Matthew Thomason. She made a mental note to make sure that when Cary was interviewed further, Mac would ask him the names of the two guests from Boston.

"Say," Cary said, with a hesitant manner. "I heard a rumor around town that the man playing poker actually died. Is that true? He sure looked sick when I saw him crumple up like that."

"He did die," Brenda said, not offering further details. "I guess the town is buzzing about it."

Cary looked shaken, but Brenda saw that his eyes remained calm as he spoke. "I had no idea he was dead when I saw it all happen. The detective spent time checking him over until the paramedics came. We were shooed to the side to give the paramedics room and I presumed they took him to the hospital to recover." He shook his head as if in disbelief.

"Yes, very sad. But these things happen. It certainly was sudden." She watched for his reaction, but his face seemed blank. "Well, enough about town gossip. I came to welcome you to the Sweetfern Harbor family, and to thank you for your help during the gala. I hope you'll let your real estate customers know they can always come stay at my bed and breakfast if they need a place to stay while they look for a new house."

Brenda bid him farewell and headed for the police station. She had plenty to share with Mac and the chief. Bob told her to join him in Mac's office. He closed the door and Brenda told them everything she had learned about Cary Buckley.

"I don't think he has any intentions of selling real estate here. Who sets up a real estate office downtown without a sign, a phone, or a computer? It's nothing but a front to find a way into the gala. I don't think he's telling the truth about what he knows. I didn't ask him about his former last name, Thomason, but he seemed pretty cagey when I asked him about the two guests he knew from Boston. Has anyone contacted them yet?" Mac shook his head. Brenda continued. "I think it was simply luck that he came into Sweet Treats the very day Hope's delivery person was out for a family emergency. It proved to be an easy way to get into the party." She was not finished. "It relieved him of figuring how to get in without an invitation, I guess. We checked tickets at the door pretty carefully."

The two men leaned back in their chairs. Mac clasped his fingers and nodded. "You are probably right about that, but there is no proof he killed Matthew Thomason."

"It's true that there isn't any proof yet," Brenda said, "but when the lab results come back from all of those samples you'll be closer. Did you have the lab check the samples from Matthew's drink first? The red wine bottles and glasses?"

Mac assured them that samples had been taken from every opened bottle of liquor, plus food not consumed. Chief Ingram asked her why that was important.

"Matthew ordered a good stout red wine. Those were his words, according to the server I spoke to yesterday afternoon on the phone. She was the one who brought it to him. She was a temporary hire for that night but I tracked her down. She said she picked up a tray with varied drinks on it. According to her, Cary told her someone ordered a red wine and just to ask who it was for. Apparently, he said he wasn't sure which guest ordered wine. She is broken up and convinced it was that wine that poisoned him. She thinks his death is all her fault."

"We'll need to get her down here to question her further," Mac said.

"She'll be down around one this afternoon and you'll have your chance then."

"I'm going to put a tail on Cary Buckley," Mac said. He thanked Brenda for moving so fast on the background research. "I have a lot more to discuss with you, but wait a second while I send an undercover officer to mosey down by that new real estate office."

The chief and Brenda chatted about the investigation until Mac returned.

"That's about all we can do for now. We'll know Cary's every move soon enough. I wonder if he had an accomplice. Did you see anyone acting unusual last night, Brenda?"

"It was hard to tell with so many people mingling, and of course everyone wore masks." Her eyebrows wrinkled and then she looked up in shock. "Wait—I did hear a name that sounded familiar. At least, familiar after my internet search. I heard someone ask a lovely lady about her husband Arthur. Arthur Blodgett was on the guest list, I remember seeing his name there."

"We'll have to get him back from Boston and question him, too," Chief Ingram told his detective, who nodded and made a note.

Brenda told them more about the messy ending of the business partnership between Arthur and Matthew. "There were bitter lawsuits and counter-suits filed so many years ago, I would imagine that Arthur has some lingering motive, or at least ill will toward his former business partner. We need to know more about him, and figure out if he might have worked with Cary in any way."

Bob and Mac were deep into conversation about how to prioritize the many leads when Brenda glanced at her watch. It read eleven forty-five. Hungry and needing some time to think, she left the men to their chat and went to the small police station kitchen. In the refrigerator, she managed to find deli meat and sliced cheese. She carefully checked the sell-by date on the mayonnaise jar before she spread it onto slices of bread from the loaf she found in the cabinet. You could never be too sure with the police station fridge; one time she found some mustard in there that was three years past its expiration date. There was no lettuce in the fridge, but she did find three lunch-sized bags of chips in the cupboard. She stacked it all on a tray which she then took to the chief's office. Bob and Mac looked up, surprised and grateful, then immediately set to the food.

She offered to get iced tea or lemonade from the refrigerator but the clerk beat her to it, stepping in with an amused look. "I thought you'd like cold drinks along with those sandwiches," said the clerk. "Be careful Brenda," she added with a chuckle, "you're going to spoil them."

Brenda rolled her eyes. "Better spoiled than starving. We have to solve this case."

After the clerk left, the three discussed the case until it was time to greet Lynn Tucker, the server. She was slight of frame, and Brenda's impression was that if a strong wind caught her, she would be gone forever. Wispy blonde hair hung over one eye, and her hands shook. Brenda reassured her that the police just wanted to hear her story. Lynn again expressed her guilt, convinced she had served poisoned wine.

"You had no way of knowing if a drink you served had poison in it," she said. "Try to relax and just tell the detective what you told me on the phone. Besides, no one knows yet whether the poison was in that wine or somewhere else when he ingested it."

Her shoulders relaxed and Brenda led her to the interrogation room. They had decided one officer questioning the frail young woman was enough, although a second, female officer stood just inside the door. Mac had a knack for knowing how to relax people he deemed innocent when asking questions. His expertise worked with Lynn. She told him exactly what had happened from the time she picked up the drink tray until she served the first table.

"Cary told me to make sure someone got the wine. He didn't know who asked for it and told me to find out. I presumed it was one of the women, since women tend to order wine more often than the hard stuff. But the older gentleman signaled it was for him and so I—set the glass down in front of him." Her hands trembled. "I don't know anything else. I was just there to earn money. I'm old enough serve drinks."

She reached into her pocket and produced her driver's license before Mac had time to tell her it wasn't necessary. He took it and verified her age, then handed it back to her. She continued. "I'm really upset that I delivered the poison to that man. Mrs. Rivers told me no one is sure it was the wine that killed him, but I heard he slumped over right after taking a sip or two."

"Did you have any way of knowing there was poison in any of the drinks?" She shook her head vigorously. "Then you didn't poison the man. Someone else did that and we're going to find out who it was."

Mac excused Lynn Tucker after asking her a few basic background questions. She told him she lived on the outskirts of Sweetfern Harbor. Her father was a commercial fisherman and her mother washed clothes and kept house for a well-off family known around town. Lynn, age twenty-three, found odd jobs to support a two-year old child while living at home with her parents.

Mac got a call on his cell when he left the interrogation room. It was the officer assigned to follow Cary Buckley.

"Do you want to go down to the Octopus Tavern with me?" he asked Brenda.

She looked at Chief Ingram, who shrugged his shoulders. "I doubt a bona fide realtor has a few drinks in the middle of his workday," he said. They laughed, as Brenda grabbed her purse.

She and Mac got into her car and he drove them down to the tavern. "My officer tailed him to the bar. This will probably be his undoing. Once a culprit starts drinking, the truth tends to come out, one way or another."

"It's a little early for drinking. It's the middle of the afternoon."

"We'll, you're in for a surprise then, when we see several in the bar doing just that when we get there."

"I'm glad I'm not a heavy drinker or I'd never keep the bed and breakfast running smoothly," Brenda said.

"You're too passionate about your work, to get getting soused in the middle of the day. That's why I love you," Mac said with a chuckle. He reached over and squeezed her hand.

Brenda recognized the SUV she had seen parked in front of Cary's new office. "He's here for sure," she told Mac. "That's the SUV I saw at his office."

They hesitated just inside the tavern, so their eyes could adjust to the darker room. Both saw Cary Buckley sitting at the bar. Brenda's bed and breakfast guest, Jack McAuliffe, sat next to him. A thousand thoughts raced through Brenda's head. She recalled several times when her young guest declined to join his wife and her two new friends when they wanted to explore Sweetfern Harbor. Mac noted the look on Brenda's face. He pulled her just inside the coatroom near the doorway, out of earshot of anyone inside.

"What is it, Brenda?"

"I must be jumping to conclusions, there is no way Jack McAuliffe is involved with Cary Buckley, yet there they sit together."

"They could simply be enjoying a drink together. That doesn't prove Jack came down here with him. My officer didn't mention anyone in the SUV with Cary."

It took Mac's practical conclusion to calm Brenda. "I guess you're right. I've seen nothing about Jack McAuliffe that tells me he could possibly be involved in a crime of any kind."

"Let's sit at that table against the wall. It will put us close enough to eavesdrop."

The server, Tilly, had begun work at the Octopus the day she turned twenty-one, and now at forty-six, she knew everyone who came into the bar, unless they were tourists passing through. She recognized Mac and Brenda, but before she could greet them, she caught Mac's warning look. He put his finger over his lips briefly, signaling her not to call him by name. So far, neither Cary nor Jack had noticed the detective and Brenda come in.

Tilly went behind the bar and filled two glasses of iced coke and set them on the table. She smiled at Mac and

Brenda and said in a hushed tone, "Welcome to the Octopus." She was used to acting with discretion, especially when a police officer appeared at the same time as two out of towners at the bar.

Cary and Jack continued to enjoy the drinks before them without words. As Brenda and Mac watched covertly, Cary ordered two more drinks in the time that Jack stuck with the one. From where they sat, the walls of their booth hid them well enough that they could watch unobtrusively.

It seemed that Jack had noted Cary's balance on the bar stool was steadily declining. He started to caution the man on ordering a third, but Cary started mumbling.

Jack attempted to distract him and rein him back into a normal conversation. The one thing they had in common was that they both had attended the masquerade gala.

"So, Buckley, I saw you had some time off at the big party the other night, did you have a little fun in the middle of your work?"

Cary's words slurred. "I just took that gig to get into the big party. Sometimes I have good luck that way." His left leg began to slide from his seating. He shifted back onto the bar stool. "It was a good party, for sure. At least I had fun. I'm not sure about that dead man. He was murdered, you know."

Jack's head jerked toward his companion. By now,

Brenda knew Jack had never met Cary Buckley until now. It was sheer opportunity that he sat next to her suspect, and more so that she and Mac sat in a strategic place to hear the entire conversation.

"Yep, he's dead as a doornail for sure. I'm glad, you know? He didn't deserve to live. He used to be a high and mighty man. Did you know that?"

Jack shook his head but did not answer, shocked at the statement.

CHAPTER EIGHT

CHILDHOOD LOSSES

*J*ack McAuliffe remained glued to the bar stool next to Cary Buckley. The last thing he wanted to do was stick around with a drunk. He merely stopped in to have a quick drink before going back to join his wife at the B & B. He hoped Emily would be there. He loved her deeply and wanted to spend more time with her. He understood her drive to befriend anyone who needed her help, and that didn't bother him at all. But he was hoping she would spend the rest of their stay with him.

Jack listened to the man next to him rambling on while he ran several scenarios through his mind, deciding how best to escape gracefully.

"Did you hear me? I said that man deserved to die. Too

bad it wasn't a worse death, though." He splashed his drink down the front of his shirt.

Jack turned to leave without answering, and then Brenda and Mac for the first time. Mac again pressed his finger to his lips and signaled for Jack to stay. The detective was sure Cary Buckley would spill important details at any moment. Jack began to get nervous, but he understood the signal and turned back to his inebriated companion.

"Why do you say he didn't deserve to live?"

"Because I know who he was. He was my own father. Can you believe that? He abandoned his own family to starve. He left us without a penny, took all of his money with him. Can you believe that?"

Jack's stomach turned, increasingly sure he sat next to a murderer. If the detective was not sitting behind him, he would have left the tavern before he lost not only his drink, but his breakfast and lunch as well. He wasn't sure he could continue this and wished the detective would just arrest the guy right now. He took a few deep breaths, and it dawned on him the man hadn't actually confessed to murdering anyone. He merely held a grudge against the man who he said was his father.

"Wait, I thought your last name is Buckley. I understood the man who died was named Matthew Thomason. Why don't you share his name?"

Cary's drink sloshed to the rim. His eyes resembled cold

steel and he appeared to sober up. "He was my father only because he contributed to my conception. I got rid of that last name the first chance I got. My stepfather was a real father to me. He gave me his last name and it has served me well over the years. I didn't need the worthless name Thomason in my ancestry." He took a long swig of the drink and pushed it toward the bartender for more. The man looked at Cary and decided the next drink would be watered down considerably.

Jack had no idea what to say after that declaration. He was no interrogator. Luckily, Jack was spared from trying to figure out how to get the man to talk more.

"You know something? My own so-called father didn't even recognize me. I took my mask off right in front of him when I was in the game room and still he didn't even know me."

"I didn't see you playing cards in there."

Cary chose to ignore the statement.

"I know who killed him. He was killed, you know. Do you want to know how I know that?" He didn't wait for Jack to answer. He simply leaned in with a sneer and said with a breathy swagger, "I killed him. It was me. It was so easy pretending to be a bartender. I asked for that job for a reason. It was the easiest way to get the deed done. You want something done—you gotta do it y'rself..."

Mac called for back-up, leaning down to speak into his

mobile so even Brenda could barely hear him. Meanwhile, Jack left the bar and headed for the bathroom with a sickened look on his face. As Brenda watched, the detective made the decision that a drunk Cary was no match for Mac's own sober strength, and he walked over and easily snapped the handcuffs on the drunken customer. He read the man his rights and informed him he was being charged with murder, then swiftly handed him over to officers from the cover unit he had requested, who had just arrived on scene.

Mac and Brenda turned to head to the parking lot, planning to follow the patrol car back to the police station. Mac hesitated and Brenda turned to look at him with a question in her eyes.

"I want to talk with Jack a minute when he comes out of the restroom."

Jack's ashen face told her how shaken he was over the encounter. Mac thanked him for his help and told him they would need a witness statement, since he had heard the confession first-hand.

"Do you want me to drive you back to the Bed and Breakfast, Jack?" Brenda asked the bartender for a glass of cold water for Jack. He accepted it and took a long drink.

"I'll be all right. I do need to catch up with Emily, unless she's out shopping again." He attempted a weak laugh.

"I heard her tell Maddie and Susan she planned to find a good book and read in the sitting room."

"That's good," Jack said. "I could use a little moral support just now." He promised to come down to the station later that afternoon and provide a full statement.

Once back at the station, two officers were sent to Cary's cell with a pot of black coffee to help sober him up. Mac glanced at his watch.

"I'll give him about a half-hour and start in on him. I'm not so sure he acted alone."

Brenda had to agree with him, but neither had any ideas on that, unless there was involvement by Arthur Blodgett, Matthew's former partner. For now, they would have to hear from Cary.

"I hope he doesn't pass out before you get to him," she said.

"He won't be going anywhere. It might actually be a good thing to let him sleep it off and then start with him when he wakes up."

The officers reported to Mac that Cary Buckley was out cold. "He kept mumbling about his life way back when he was a kid. Something about being so poor he didn't even have a doorman." The officers laughed. "We have no idea what that's all about, but he was pretty well socked out when we brought him in. He wouldn't even drink the coffee."

Mac agreed. "Let him sleep it off. There's plenty of time to get the truth out of him. There are three witnesses to his confession at the bar."

Brenda told Mac she should get back to her guests. "This is the last day for most of them."

"I'll see you later. You know, Cary must hold real grudges," Mac said. "He probably never got over being left destitute by his father. The doorman comment must refer to his childhood—didn't you say his father lived in a penthouse in New York?"

"I'm sure those memories are embedded in his mind to this day," she paused. "You may want to make sure you ask Cary who the couple is that he knew in Boston. They were at the party and I'm fairly certain it was his father's old business partner, Arthur Blodgett. It would be interesting to know how the two of them are connected."

When Brenda drove up the long drive to her Queen Anne bed and breakfast, she relaxed, happy for the respite. She chose to go in the front entrance where Allie greeted her cheerfully.

"It's been quiet while you were out—everyone is happy doing their own thing," she announced. "Emily McAuliffe has been in the sitting room all afternoon reading. Maddie and Susan went back downtown. Jack came in a little while ago and he and Emily went up to their room."

"Thanks for the update. I'm glad everyone is enjoying their stay. Is Phyllis here?"

"She and William just left a few minutes ago. She said she would be back to help with dinner tonight in the dining room."

"Could you call and tell her to take the rest of the evening off? She and William could probably use some down time together."

That evening, Maddie and Susan wore smiles when they entered the dining room. "We've had a wonderful time this entire weekend," Maddie told Brenda. "I'm going to start saving money for another visit. We're still talking about the masquerade gala. We had never been to one before and it was so much fun."

Brenda had to smile at their consistent enthusiasm.

"We have had a lovely time," Susan said. "I have a feeling we'll be back again. Jack told us about the July boat races that are celebrated in Sweetfern Harbor. That would be a good summertime getaway."

Emily and Jack heard the conversation and Jack told everyone they planned to come back during the boat race weekend as well.

"He's hoping that one day he'll be good enough to compete," Emily said, with a fond smile.

"I'm good enough now," Jack countered. "I just need practice and more speed."

The dinner consisted of a choice of sockeye salmon or seared steaks. The sisters and most guests chose the salmon. Conversations flowed easily and the diners drifted into the sitting room after dinner for their last after dinner gathering. Brenda left them with the promise that she would see each one before they left the next morning.

For the first time in a while, Brenda's exhaustion lessened to the point of allowing her to peacefully relax before sleep that night. She hoped Mac would be home soon. There wasn't much he could do until Cary Buckley slept off his drunkenness. Just as she was ready to climb into bed, Mac came through the front sitting area. She left the bedside lamp on and greeted him when he stuck his head in the bedroom doorway.

"I'm so glad you're home at a decent time," Brenda said. "Let's forget this entire investigation and get some sleep."

"I'm ready to sleep through a whole night. I've almost forgotten what that feels like."

The detective's face showed faint lines, like a map that had been pencil-drawn. He got ready for bed and climbed in next to Brenda. Both nestled together, knowing their home was right there, as long as they were together.

At one in the morning, Mac's cell rang. It took a few seconds for him to awaken enough to answer it.

"How did that happen?" he asked the caller. Brenda turned over and listened to the one-sided conversation.

When Mac ended the call, he flicked on the bedside lamp and looked down at his wife. He groaned and flopped back on his pillow. Brenda asked about the call.

"Someone came into the police station around eleven and asked to talk with someone in the holding cells. Cary Buckley, of course. The jailer told him he would have to come back in the morning. There was an argument and the visitor shoved the jailer against the wall and knocked him out. He must have taken the keys from him. Just that fast, the assailant opened Cary's cell and got him out the back door. They escaped."

"Why are you just finding out about it?"

"Two night shift officers had been out on patrol and got back to the station about fifteen minutes ago. One of them found the jailer still slumped against the wall, with a trickle of blood on the side of his face. He got the ambulance there and took the man to the hospital. In the chaos, the other officer walked down the row of cells and saw one door ajar. Cary was long gone."

Mac sat up and rubbed his head. "I can't tell you how many times I've asked for funding to add another jailer for the night shift. Our nighttime staffing is less than minimal."

He got dressed while Brenda put on some coffee. On his way out, she handed him a cup and he kissed her. "I'll keep you posted."

"Once I help the chief sort out the manhunt for Cary and this accomplice, I'm going to find out all I can about Cary's associations in Boston. Might as well, since I'm up." Brenda poured a cup of coffee for herself.

"You need to get some more sleep, Brenda. Do more research when you get up in the morning." She nodded but was too shaken by the sudden events to settle down.

Mac left and Brenda went to her computer. She pulled up Cary's name and searched for all known business contacts. She found nothing new. When she checked Matthew Thomason's name again, his former partner's name continually showed up. Arthur Blodgett was from Boston originally and had an office there still. Again, Arthur Blodgett and his wife Lily turned up no adverse postings, according to her search. Brenda decided to delve deeper into Arthur's past. She searched for the next half-hour before it led her to details on his personal life. She wondered whether the Blodgett's had children of their own. So far none were mentioned. She read that Arthur was a few years older than his former partner. His age was noted as sixty, which fit with Matthew Thomason's age.

There had to be someone connected with Cary that wanted him freed from jail.

"Who would be an accomplice in your deed?" she wondered aloud. "Was there someone at that party hiding behind a mask who helped you?"

The one thing that stuck out in Brenda's mind was the fact that Cary had apparently not recovered from the shock of losing his status as the child of wealthy parents. That much was abundantly clear from his drunken tirade and confession in the bar. Cary had been old enough to feel the full brunt of the abrupt crash into poverty. He had allowed himself to nurse a deep resentment against his father, to the point of wanting him to die. It was embedded in his psyche, and had been enough to spur him to the final, fatal act.

CHAPTER NINE

THE HUNT

*D*etective Mac Rivers walked into the police station and one of the officers met him there. He told him all he knew about the escapees, which didn't add much to what Mac had already learned on the phone. Mac asked about the injured jailer.

"I tried to wake Jim up, but he kept going in and out of consciousness. The paramedics told me he was going to be all right once he was fully awake. I couldn't get any details out of him at all except something about the man who hit him—he had a mask on."

"Did he mean like a stocking over his face or what?"

"I don't know for sure. He was just mumbling. I thought he said something about a Mardi Gras mask, like in New Orleans. He's from down there, you know."

"I didn't know that. I'm going to head for the hospital and see how he is. Hopefully, I can get something from him if he's fully awake by now. Did you send your partner with him?"

"He's there standing guard on Jim's hospital room. I told him you would let him know if you wanted him to stay there or not. It's too bad we only have one other person jailed. I asked the guy in the holding cell down the hall, but he told me he didn't hear anything. He slept through it all, so he's no help."

On the way to the hospital, Mac's first and only thought was that the Mardi Gras mask sounded exactly like the masks worn at the masquerade gala. He called Brenda while driving, knowing she was at her computer, despite his advice to go back to bed. She answered right away and he told her the latest.

"I'll see if Jim can talk to me. He can give me a description of the man's physique at least, and maybe tell me if he picked up anything that would be significant—cologne or tattoos on the hands, something. Chief Ingram has a separate team out combing through town, and an APB was sent to the state police, too."

"Hopefully it won't be long before Cary's nabbed, right along with his accomplice."

"I'll let you know what I find out. In the meantime, get back to bed."

"When pigs fly."

"Not even a snowball's chance in—?"

Brenda laughed, cutting him off. "Exactly. I love you."

Mac returned the sentiment and ended the call as he arrived at the wing of the hospital where Jim was being cared for. When he walked down the hall, he saw the officer on guard.

"He's awake, Detective. I haven't asked him any questions. The nurses have been in and out since the doctor looked him over. I don't think he was seriously hurt."

"Stay here until further notice. Make sure nobody gets in here without my say-so."

Mac headed into the room. Jim tried to sit up and Mac encouraged him to stay where he was. When Jim assured him that he was well enough to go over the incident, Mac started with his questions.

"Did you get a good look at him before he knocked you out, Jim."

"That's the thing, I'm not so sure it was a he. I smelled some kind of a perfume or a lotion more like what a woman would wear." He averted his eyes from Mac. "If it was a woman who knocked me out cold I'll be the laughing stock of the police station." Mac told him to forget that and go on. "Well, I was sitting at the desk at the end of the hall when it happened. Right where I'm usually stationed during my shift, like always, you know? I heard someone come in through the back door. I just thought the night shift guys were coming in that way and didn't pay any attention. I was wide awake, playing a game of solitaire. A normal, quiet night. I stood up to stretch and put the cards aside. I couldn't seem to win even one game. You ever had a night like that, playing a losing game of cards?" The man seemed embarrassed and focused on the card game as if it would distract from what happened next.

"Jim, you'll have to get to the point if we're going to catch whoever did it. We know you're not at fault. But we need to get Cary and his partner and crime into custody, so just tell me what happened, please."

"Okay. Sorry Detective, I get carried away at times. Anyway, I shuffled the cards back into the deck and turned around. Before I realized it wasn't a cop, a baseball bat came flying toward me. The only thing I remember is that it was a tall person, probably like five ten or so, dark hair. But I couldn't see their face. It was masked, and not the type of cheap disguise that some criminals choose. It reminded me of something people wear when they celebrate Mardi Gras down in New Orleans where I grew up. It covered the whole face except for part of the mouth." He paused, wincing at the memory of the baseball bat. "Now that I think about it, the mouth made me think it was a woman, too. No signs of shaving around the chin like you'd see on a man. Of course, it all happened in a split second."

"They told me you said someone asked to see the prisoner, and there was an altercation."

Jim looked puzzled, then troubled. "I must be out of my head, they knocked me so hard. I swear I only heard the noise from the back. I don't remember anything about someone asking to see the prisoner. I would have told them to come back in the morning anyway, that's procedure. But maybe my memory's bad, Mac. I took quite a shot."

Mac stepped out into the hall and called for a sketch artist to come at daylight to draw Jim's description. He went back into the hospital room.

"What size baseball bat are you talking about?"

"It looked like a kid's bat. It wasn't big enough to be handled by a big-time baseballer." Jim pressed his hand against his forehead and groaned. Mac told him to lie still and try to rest. Pondering the conflicting stories he had heard, Mac left the man and stepped out into the hall to take some notes.

It was still the middle of the night and Brenda's eyes were heavy from lack of sleep. She was almost ready to take Mac's advice when she decided to search Arthur Blodgett's profile again. This time she clicked on a foreign language link, hoping the automatic translation function on her web browser would kick in. She was right —and she could now read an article about his family that she hadn't seen before. Suddenly, she was wide awake. Lily and Arthur had children after all—four of them, all grown. They each graduated from prestigious universities in the eastern part of the United States. Three were male and one female. All spoke fluent French, their mother's native tongue, and the family had enjoyed time in a villa outside Paris for years.

Brenda wondered where Mac was and finally decided to call him.

"Did you check out the background of that server we interviewed, Lynn Tucker? The one who said she lives at home with a small child?"

"I didn't. I gave the information to Bryce. I can check with him. What's up?"

"Probably nothing at all," Brenda said. "I just found that the Blodgett's have a daughter named Lynn. It might be a silly coincidence. Lots of people are named Lynn. Besides, Lynn Tucker doesn't look like she comes from wealth."

Mac did not say anything. Brenda waited.

"Nothing is silly at this point in time, Brenda. I'm going to give Bryce an early wake-up call in about a half-hour. I'll ask him if he's had time to look into Lynn Tucker. There could be another connection there. After all, even if she's not related to the Blodgett's, she did serve the drink to the dead man."

"When are you going to come home and get some sleep?"

"Probably not until later this afternoon. I'll try to get some shut-eye then. Hopefully by that time we'll have Cary Buckley back in custody, right along with whoever sprang him from jail."

The detective stuck to his plan to get Bryce up earlier than usual. He told him what had happened a few hours earlier. They met in Mac's office with Chief Ingram and quickly laid out plans to intensify the manhunt. Bryce told Mac he found nothing about Lynn Tucker except the fact that Brenda had her on the list of employees at the gala.

"I searched briefly for a Lynn Tucker as I did the others on the list. Several Lynn Tuckers came up but none fit her description. I mean, the ones I saw were older than she is."

They switched to the problem at hand. Officers were directed to their search areas for the escaped man. Word was already buzzing around Sweetfern Harbor that Cary Buckley had been arrested for Matthew Thomason's murder. It was not long before news of his jail break swarmed through the town as well. Hope Williams paled when she heard the news, and it hit her that Brenda's instincts about him had been on target. Hope knew her friend had suspected something unusual about the sudden appearance of the man in their little town.

Downtown, Cary's office was locked, and when officers forced their way in, they found it empty. Worried about the scope of the manhunt, Mac sent bulletins out as far away as New York City and Boston.

Arthur Blodgett knew he had to come clean with what he knew about Cary Buckley. It was only a matter of time before the cops would question him. He sat with Lily and explained everything. Arthur swore to her that he thought Cary only meant to make Matthew suffer a stomach ailment from the drink.

"I would have done everything in my power to stop him from killing Matthew had I only known that was his intention." Lily was in agreement that there was only one thing to do. He left their comfortable Boston house to drive to the Sweetfern Harbor police station.

On the way, he thought about how Cary had allowed bitterness to overtake all rational thought. He had seen that the young man clung to resentment when they spoke after many years of not seeing one another, but he never would have guessed that Cary would throw away his future with this act of violent revenge.

Arthur breathed a sigh of relief that the disturbed man had not married his daughter Lynn. At one time the two had met by accident and cultivated a friendship, until it was almost too late. Thankfully, eventually realized they had become more than friends. She knew about the severed connection between Arthur and Matthew, and who Cary was, and didn't want her daughter becoming entangled. She stepped in and finally convinced Lynn to break it off with Cary. It had not been a pretty ending.

Now, Arthur would come clean with what he knew of Cary's actions the night of the masquerade gala and put the whole messy business behind him once and for all.

Cary Buckley ran for his life, still stumbling from his recent hangover. As they switched to a new car to avoid being tailed, his rescuer pushed a thick wad of bills into his hands. All he knew is that they were headed for a private plane bound for Europe, and he was desperate to make his escape.

When Mac leaned back in his chair he ran his fingers through thick blondish hair that held a few strands of grey. Chief Ingram told him to go home and get some sleep. A few leads were turned in on sightings of the escaped prisoner and his accomplice, and law enforcement was doing everything they could.

"We'll get him soon, Mac. I'll call you if anything significant develops."

Mac knew he needed sleep and headed for Sheffield Bed and Breakfast, calling Brenda on his way. When he came up to the apartment, she had a tray of hot food ready for him. He ate it all and then kissed her. The bed was turned down, just waiting for him.

Brenda had napped a bit off and on all day and while Mac slept, she now delved deeper into exactly who Lynn Tucker was. She finally closed the computer and picked up her car keys.

"You can get me by cell," she told Allie and Phyllis. "Mac is sleeping and I'm going to see if I can go find Lynn Tucker."

"I know who she is," Phyllis said. Brenda jerked her head around and asked what she knew. "She's had a hard time of it. She got involved with a no-gooder and ended up pregnant. Her parents took their daughter in—she's their only child, you see—and she seems to be getting back on her feet. That's why I was so glad to see her working here at the gala, she's come so far. Why do you need to see her?"

Brenda's response was a weary smile. "I suppose there is no need." The information from Phyllis was good corroboration. There were still questions to be answered, but she wasn't too worried. Perhaps she could lie down to rest a little after all.

When she walked back into her apartment she heard Mac's phone ring. He picked it up and then got out of bed. "They've got him, Brenda." He told her someone saw Cary as they drove past a private airport earlier. The witness saw the man with a second person, someone tall, who was directing him toward a small private plane getting ready to take off. Luckily, they called in the sighting and the police were able to intervene before the plane was cleared for takeoff.

"Where was the plane going?"

"The FAA said the pilot had filed a flight plan since they were headed overseas. To a private airfield at a villa in France, just outside Paris."

Brenda gasped. "The Blodgett's have a villa there. That can't be a coincidence. Someone from that family helped him escape and was planning to send him off to Europe."

Mac's phone rang again and after listening he told the

caller to talk to Brenda. She put the phone on speaker so they could both listen in.

"Hello, Brenda," Bryce said. "I thought you might like to know this, since you were the one who was curious about her background. It turns out that Lynn Blodgett is the one who got Cary out of jail. We caught her only a mile away from the private airport. The two of them were going to fly separately to avoid suspicion, and once in France they planned to marry and live there."

Bryce went on to describe Lynn as a tall, athletic woman who had no problem overcoming Jim at the jail. The baseball bat she used had been recovered in the trunk of a car registered to her but left abandoned in a parking lot. It had Jim's blood on it, as well as her fingerprints, so they had her dead to rights. Both Lynn and Cary were in custody.

"There's more. Arthur Blodgett left his house in Boston just before these two were captured," Bryce said. "The chief has called him back in. He wants to know more about Arthur himself, of course, but now we're also wondering exactly what he knew and the suspicious timing of his road trip. We'll get to the bottom of it all."

Brenda and Mac exchanged glances, knowing how satisfied the young detective must feel at the moment. It was plain to hear in his voice. They all felt a measure of relief, even knowing there were still the interrogations to get through.

After they ended the call, Mac was wide awake. "I'm going down to help with the interrogations. Do you want to join me to see it all through to the end?" Mac asked.

"You know I do," Brenda said.

CHAPTER TEN

WRAPPING UP

*a*rthur Blodgett drove to Sweetfern Harbor, ready to tell everything he knew about Cary and his birth father, but still wary. He had no intention of spilling details about how he had been the cause of Matthew Thomason's financial difficulties long after the business partnership was dissolved. He told himself there was no reason to divulge that since it was a whole different matter. He frowned, remembering Chief Ingram's call while he was already on his way to the small town, telling him to come back to the police station for further questioning. It was just like law enforcement in a town like Sweetfern Harbor, thinking businessman like him had nothing better to do, he thought. He decided not to let on that he was already headed to Sweetfern Harbor for his own reasons of conscience.

Arthur parked his car and got out, just as Brenda and

Mac arrived. They nodded at one another when Brenda hurried ahead and introduced herself.

"I don't believe we met at the masquerade gala. I'm Brenda Rivers, the owner of the Sheffield Bed and Breakfast. I hope you enjoyed your evening with us that night."

"My wife Lily and I had a very good time. I'm not sure what this business down here is all about," he said, glancing at his Rolex. "I have meetings later this evening, so I hope whatever this is about won't take long." Arthur wasn't sure how to bring up the issue of what he knew about Cary's plans, but trusted it would come up sooner or later.

Mac caught up with them. His eyes bored into Arthur Blodgett's and neither man spoke. Mac held the station door for Brenda, followed by Arthur, who was immediately escorted into an interrogation room. The chief and Bryce came in and sat down. While they grilled Arthur about what he saw at the party and how he knew the deceased man, Mac and a female officer went into the room where Lynn Blodgett sat waiting.

She was poised and calm. Her flawless skin showed no signs of tension. Brenda watched through the one-way mirror. Lynn answered questions truthfully with her lawyer next to her. Several times he stopped her, but for the most part she did not appear worried about going to jail. Brenda decided money gave her that assurance, and nothing else. Lynn Blodgett must be clueless about how much trouble she was in, Brenda thought. A few hours later, much to Mac's chagrin, the judge allowed her to post bail until her court date.

Mac and the chief, along with Brenda, moved to the third room where Cary Buckley sat. Brenda pulled up a chair at the end of the table. Cary and his lawyer sat on one side of the table with the two officers across from them. Cary's attorney didn't allow him to answer many of the questions posed to him, and Mac and Bob soon decided they weren't going to get much farther with their questioning that day. The judge didn't grant him bail since he had already escaped from a jail cell once, and was considered to be a high risk to flee the country again. If he had been female, and from a prestigious family, he may have fared better, Brenda thought.

Next, Brenda, Mac and Chief Ingram joined Arthur Blodgett. When Arthur was informed of his daughter Lynn's involvement in the jail break, his reaction was one of disbelief. "My wife saw to it that they parted company long ago," he said. "There is no way she could be involved with him, or involved with a crime like this. Cary Buckley was simply a poor match for her and she came to realize that."

"She has confessed, with her lawyer present. I don't think she quite understands the depth of the trouble she's in, Mr. Blodgett. She and Cary planned to fly to France separately, marry there and settle in for life. Your daughter is involved, and very deeply," Mac said. "The question is, how much of a part did you play in arranging for one of your private jets to whisk them off?"

Arthur sputtered. "My daughter often asks to fly in one of them. The manager of my planes simply let me know that she planned to fly to our villa in France. Of course I said it was fine. In fact, I'm in the process of turning one of the jets over to her control. She shouldn't need to ask my permission for anything now. Lynn no longer lives at home. She's on her own and runs a subsidiary of my main textile business." He glared at the officers. "She's smart enough not to jeopardize what she has going for her."

"She wasn't smart this time," the chief said.

"Was she at the gala?" Brenda asked.

It was as if Arthur noticed her presence in the room for the first time. He wondered why the owner of a bed and breakfast was sitting in on a police interrogation, but he let that go by.

"No. Or if she was there, neither my wife nor I saw her, and we stayed through most of the night. Of course, with the large crowd there, and everyone wearing masks, I suppose I could have simply not seen her. She never came to speak to me, and I'm sure my wife would have told me if she'd seen her."

"She was on the invitation list and answered her R.S.V.P.

I presumed she came, though I have to admit I didn't meet one on one with every guest," Brenda said.

Arthur looked at her with curiosity and wanted to ask what her part was in the questioning, but his lawyer interrupted.

"If that is all for now, officers, my client and I will be on our way." He stood up and signaled for Arthur to do the same.

"Your client knowingly allowed someone to cause illness in another, so that is an issue we'll have to address soon. Accessory to a felony charge of intent to harm, not to mention murder. But that's all for now," the chief said, with a carefully neutral tone. "Stay in touch. We may need you back in here."

"I'll be in New York on business. You can contact me through my lawyer from now on," Arthur said.

Stone-faced, the lawyer handed the chief his business card and both men walked out. The only thing on Arthur's mind now was how to tell his wife of the deep trouble their only daughter had gotten mixed up in. The issue of his conscience, where Cary was concerned, had faded from his mind entirely.

Brenda was first to speak after the men left. "My take is that he's told us what he knows. I get the feeling he and his daughter are not all that close if they didn't even connect at the party," she said. "I still wonder what caused him to dissolve his partnership in the business with Matthew."

"I think that can be left to the lawyers to sort out, though it is curious," the chief said. "Hard to say what all goes on behind closed doors in big companies like that."

"It could be relevant down the road." The chief nodded agreement.

Once Cary was secured in his cell and both Arthur and Lynn Blodgett and their attorneys had left, the officers and Brenda returned to Mac's office. They discussed the interrogations. The conclusion was that there was enough evidence to as the District Attorney for an indictment and trial for Cary Buckley. As for Lynn and Arthur Blodgett, there was more work to be done to determine their involvement and the exact charges. A plan needed to be well thought out.

Brenda and Mac arrived home in time to enjoy dinner with guests. Phyllis and William joined them. The mood was light and William offered the guests a variety of suggestions to enjoy the area. Several were interested in going to the beach since the early springtime was beginning to warm the air somewhat.

"Don't expect to swim yet," William said. "The water is still quite cold."

A young couple told the story of once participating in a Polar Bear Dip in December. With laughter, they emphasized it was their first and last experience with such a feat.

Brenda and Mac left them in the sitting room after much lively conversation, then retired upstairs. For the first time in several days, they slept soundly.

———

The next morning, Hope Williams arrived at the bed and breakfast to deliver a batch of freshly baked pastries from Sweet Treats. She entered the kitchen through the back door, and asked Chef Morgan if Brenda was up yet.

"She's in there finishing up with coffee. She and Phyllis are just going over things that need to be done. You can go on in. I'm sure they won't mind."

Hope pushed open the swinging doors that led to the beverage nook. From there she went through the doorway to the dining room. She poured a cup of coffee from the carafe on the buffet and joined the two women, who happily turned to greet her.

Hope smiled apologetically. "Brenda, I want to tell you how sorry I am that I unwittingly hired a criminal to deliver the desserts the other night."

Brenda reached for her hand. "Hope, you couldn't have known. None of us did. There is nothing to apologize for. You needed a delivery person in a pinch and he took advantage of it. That's all there is to it. Cary came across as very personable. He was intent on a sinister purpose, and would have found a way to get in to the party, one way or another."

"I think he had a very hard childhood," Phyllis said. "You know that his wealthy father left his family with nothing. What a mean man he must have been." She shook her head in consternation. "They must have really suffered in poverty."

"His mother had drive though," Brenda said. "She pulled herself up and made something of the situation. Things turned out well for the rest of them. Cary could just never let go of the bitterness he felt for all those years."

"He must have known his father was going to be here, so his real estate license was a charade to cover his real motive." Hope sighed. "I wonder who broke him out of jail."

Brenda held back on details. She felt sure that the knowledge would somehow get out, whether she told it all or not. Only Phyllis had been the recipient of that news, and Brenda knew she could count on her best friend and confidant to keep it secret until the police were ready to make it public.

Instead, she said, "I think the police are onto all that, too. I'm sure they'll make the information public as soon as they are ready."

"Do you mean they've caught the person?" Hope's eyes widened.

"I think so, but I can't divulge that yet. There is a lot of work still to do on this case."

Hope knew from experience that Brenda was not going to budge. Even Jenny no longer passed gossip around as soon as she heard things. "Ever since Jenny married Bryce, she's become as secretive as you, Brenda. I can't get anything out of her either." Hope laughed at her own comments. "I guess if you spilled everything no crime would get solved."

Brenda reached over to pat Hope's hand again and agreed with the statement.

They enjoyed the fresh pastry until Hope said she had to get back to her shop. She had a wedding cake to design. "The bride-to-be convinced her fiancé to stop by and taste samples for his groom's cake. I'm sure that's the last thing he wants to do, but I've got samples ready for him."

Phyllis and Brenda thanked her for the treats and they began their day.

A slight-framed girl walked through the front door and with a smile, Allie asked if she could help her. She asked to speak to Brenda after introducing herself as Lynn Tucker. When Brenda came into the front area, she was surprised to see the frail young woman back at the bed and breakfast. She immediately assumed the girl wanted to ask for a permanent job.

"I heard that you may be looking for me, Mrs. Rivers."

Brenda asked her to come into her office and closed the door behind them.

"It's true, I did want to see you again. But then I discovered I had the wrong Lynn. I'm sorry if I caused you concern." The girl relaxed.

"That's a relief. I wondered if you thought I was lying, or knew more about that night than I told you already."

"Did you remember anything else?"

"I've thought and thought. The only thing I may not have told you was that I remember seeing Cary talking and dancing with a beautiful woman. She was tall and looked like someone who worked out a lot. I didn't mean to hide anything from you, I just didn't think about her until later after I kept thinking back to that night, over and over again. The woman was beautiful, and sexy. I could tell that since her gown showed a lot of her body. Her mask covered most of her face and it was so gorgeous, it must have cost a lot of money."

"Did he talk with her simply in passing, or did they have a conversation?"

"I guess both. I saw him dancing with her later. It probably doesn't mean anything, since he probably talked to a lot of beautiful guests, but I wanted to make sure I told you everything I could about that night."

"Did you ever see this woman near him when he mixed drinks at the sideboard?"

The girl thought carefully. "You know, I did see them there, right before the tray with the poisoned wine." Her eyes widened. "Do you think she put the poison in it?"

"No, let's not jump to conclusions. They were probably friends to begin with and it was simply a matter of them being together when they got the chance."

Relief reappeared on Lynn's pale face. "I'll be going now, unless you need me for anything else."

"I may need to hire you to help with the next celebration, if you'd like."

"I'd like that very much."

After Lynn Tucker left, Brenda called Mac to give him the latest addition to the scene.

CHAPTER ELEVEN

FLYING RUMORS

The sun set over the backyard later and later each evening. That night, Brenda and Mac sat in the Adirondack chairs at the edge of the garden, where seedlings turned into recognizable tiny plants. Waves lapped in sync against the seawall. Mac poured wine into two glasses and they sipped in silence.

Phyllis stood at the back door with William.

"I hate to disturb their reverie out there. Maybe we should just let them have this time together."

"I agree," William said. "We can visit later. They've had precious little time together since returning from their honeymoon last month." He pulled his own new bride close. "Let's go get some Italian food and have our own night out."

Phyllis tilted her head and William kissed her lightly.

The sun, almost hidden, continued to sink lower.

Mac stretched and yawned. "I'm glad you left Michigan and came to the ocean, Brenda."

"I'm glad too. Sometimes I have to pinch myself when I realize how generous Uncle Randolph was. I can see why he loved it so much here." She turned to Mac. "More than anything else, I'm glad I left Michigan and found you."

"Not as much as I am." He set his glass on the table and leaned over and kissed her. His lips lingered and the warmth of his love flooded through her.

They sat back again and listened to the night sounds. From nowhere, Brenda found thoughts of the masquerade gala running through her mind. Since acquiring Sheffield Bed and Breakfast, that night felt like the apex of everything she had accomplished there. Her thoughts continued to swirl, thinking about the many costumes and elaborate masks.

"I think everyone had a good time at the gala, don't you?"

Mac laughed. "If you remember the fun from that night it is something that will stay with you for a very long time. Tonight we're not going to go further than that. And yes, everyone had a good time. Even when the last dance was announced, you had the band play two more pieces. I think most people were reluctant to leave. You make an excellent hostess, Brenda. You handled everything professionally, providing a beautiful and glamorous event, but with enough personal touches to make it comfortable and warm at the same time."

"I guess I'm needy for reassurance sometimes," Brenda said.

"You are definitely not a needy person."

"I do hope the hospital asks us to do it every year. I have plenty of ideas for themes."

"I'm sure you do. Let's take a walk down by the seawall and then call it a night." Mac stood up and pulled Brenda up and pulled her to his side.

They walked hand in hand across the lawn and sat on the ledge of the wall. Mac pointed to the sky. "Look at the stars tonight. The sky is filled with them."

Brenda looked up. "Did you see that shooting star?" Her voice filled with excitement. "My dad and I used to go out and star gaze in a field owned by one of his friends who had a farm. We saw only one shooting star in all that time. It's supposed to be a sign of good things."

They star-gazed for a few more minutes, then headed back to the ornate mansion they called home. When they passed the summerhouse, Brenda reminded Mac they had to meet with a designer and get started on their new home. Mac was ready for more room and a home of their own, too. They planned to expand the summerhouse into a roomy cottage.

The next morning, Mac and Brenda awoke and got ready for the new day. They enjoyed breakfast with the guests before Mac left for work. Brenda held a morning meeting with her staff and noted areas that needed attention. She went over the roster of upcoming guests with Allie. By mid-morning, she had accomplished most of the urgent tasks and invited Phyllis to walk downtown with her.

"We can stop at Morning Sun Coffee and say hello to Molly," Brenda said. "How is she doing lately? I noticed she had a new man on her arm at the masquerade party."

"I'm so happy she's gotten back on her feet after that horrible time when Pete was arrested. I'm just glad he revealed his true colors before it was too late."

"So, who is the new man in her life?"

"His name is Jonathan Wright. He goes by Jon. He and his family have been coming here for years for vacations. He's on his own now of course, and has settled here for good. He bought a private boat dock where he rents out spaces, mainly to visitors who come with their boats." She smiled, "Seems he's quite a water enthusiast."

"Then he's come to the right place."

The women entered the coffee shop where Molly smiled broadly and waved to them. Every table was taken except for three. Brenda knew gossip flew around town and this was a good time to catch up.

"Hi Mom. How are you, Brenda?"

"I'm just fine. What's going on with you?" she asked, as Molly set steaming lattes in front of them.

"Well, things are abuzz around here. Everyone knows now that it was a woman who broke Cary Buckley out of jail. She's someone wealthy, apparently. I heard she managed to knock Jim out and get the keys. Gosh, I sure feel sorry for Jim. Everyone's making fun of him for being punched out cold by a woman, but I hear she's quite athletic and fit. I'm not sure why men think women can't do such things." She shook her head.

"Goodness. Who would do such a thing?" Phyllis asked, though she already knew from Brenda.

"Someone named Lynn Blodgett. She comes from a moneyed family in New York or Boston, I heard."

She stepped away to wait on another customer. "Looks like rumors have it right so far," Phyllis said in a quiet tone.

Molly came back not five minutes later. "One more thing.

I heard the judge let her out on bail, but she probably won't be out long. Rumor is she helped Cary poison Matthew Thomason."

"Careful with the rumors, Molly. We don't always know what is accurate," Phyllis said, in a gentle scolding tone.

Molly's face flushed pink. "I know, Mom. I'm not passing anything on, I'm just letting you know what the town is saying."

After Molly returned to her customers, Phyllis asked, "Do you think they'll get the judge to revoke her bail and re-arrest her?"

"It's possible. I'm guessing Lynn Tucker, the temporary server, said something around town about Lynn Blodgett having some part in the poisoning. To my knowledge, there is no proof of that, at least not at this point."

Both women knew there was nothing they could do to stop gossip around Sweetfern Harbor. They could only intervene if what they heard was false or unknown. Brenda was glad Mac could keep a clear head while rumors flew.

"Let's go to the police station and see if there's anything new," Brenda said.

"And accurate," Phyllis said.

Chief Bob Ingram looked up as he started for the row of cells and greeted the women. When asked, he told them so far Cary stated he was the sole killer. "He insists Lynn Blodgett had nothing to do with the murder, though he admitted she sprang him from his cell. We may never know if she helped with the poisoning that night or not."

Brenda asked if he had time to hear what Lynn Tucker told her. He stood back to allow the women to go into his office. Brenda told him of the visit. "There is no proof Lynn Blodgett did anything that night, but I think she at least knew what Cary was getting ready to do. You're right in that we may never know the truth unless Cary is pushed to tell more."

"He may do that once the reality of jail time hits him," Phyllis said.

When Brenda asked if Mac was in his office, Bob told her he'd been called to a domestic disturbance. "He should be back soon, if you want to wait."

"It's all right. We just dropped in to see if there was anything new." Brenda smiled at her friend and they left.

"I want to check on the costumes at the dry cleaners," Phyllis said. "I know they'll deliver them back to us, but I just want to check on the progress."

Brenda laughed. "You just want to make sure they haven't ruined them. You know there's no worry about that. They specialize in cleaning vintage fabrics."

"Let's stop anyway."

Brenda's cell rang. It was the hospital coordinator, thanking her again for the very successful event. "The fundraising committee is in total agreement. We'd like to make this an annual affair, and hope you'll be willing to do it again next year." Brenda assured her she would, elated at the vote of confidence.

After confirming that the costumes were in good hands, the women returned to the Sheffield Bed and Breakfast in time for a mid-afternoon snack. Allie joined them and reported on the latest guests. Most were in their twenties and thirties. Allie easily related to all of them. The three women then discussed next year's masquerade gala. That is where Mac found them when he arrived home earlier than usual.

"Don't you three ever stop with celebrations around here?" He leaned over and kissed Brenda.

"We don't," Allie said. "It takes a lot of planning to do what we do."

Mac sat down and reached for a chocolate chip cookie. He knew the women expected him to tell them something about what was going on down at the police station. He finally ended their anticipation and spoke.

"We've arrested Lynn Blodgett again after convincing the judge to revoke her bail. The chief emphasized that she had easy access to private jets and was a high-risk to flee, considering she did facilitate the escape of a prisoner. We have very good evidence on that, no matter which way the trial goes." He took a bite of the cookie, savoring it before he continued. "We'll probably bring in her father next. He knew Cary's plans to poison Matthew, but Cary tells us Arthur was in the dark about his plan to kill the man. I think he's telling the truth on that."

"These trials will have to be held in the larger of the two courtrooms downtown," Brenda said. "If anything brings the town together it's a high-profile trial. As for Lynn and her father, I expect they will each bring in a team of least three or four famous defense attorneys."

"Do you think either of them will get jail time?" Phyllis asked.

"That's hard to say," Mac said. "They will probably try for a plea deal and never spend more time in a cell. That's what a good lawyer can buy you," he said, with a grimace.

The chef came through the door with more cookies and Phyllis went to the sideboard and refilled their coffee cups. She handed Allie her usual hot tea.

"Is your father around here?" Chef Morgan asked Brenda.

"I haven't seen him this afternoon," Brenda said.

"He's out with William checking on the green," Phyllis

said. "They hope to get some golf in, but I don't know how. The ground is quite damp."

Chef Anna's face dropped a fraction and she returned to the kitchen.

"Those two have something going," Allie said. "I think we should encourage their relationship."

The other two women nodded in agreement. They laughed at Mac's befuddled expression.

"Surely you've noticed they are attracted to each other," Brenda said. She turned back to Phyllis and Allie. "Let's figure out a way they can have a dinner out together someplace." Brenda snapped her fingers. "Morgan told me that she played golf with her brother years ago. Maybe if I tell my father she likes golf that could be a good starting point to move them along."

Mac stood up and shrugged. He walked away, shaking his head and wondering if somehow the women were responsible for nabbing him and William in their recent marriages. At the doorway, he shook his head again and looked back at Brenda.

That would not have been possible, he knew. Mac was attracted to Brenda almost from the day she arrived in Sweetfern Harbor to assume ownership of Sheffield Bed and Breakfast. True, she exasperated him at first, but once they learned to trust one another, it was true love all the way.

He vowed to have no part in their plans. Mac realized that this was simply the other side of Brenda's amazing detective skills, however. She loved to solve crimes and puzzle through mysteries, almost as much as she loved solving relationships and matchmaking, and he loved her for it all the more.

ABOUT THE AUTHOR

Wendy Meadows is an emerging author of cozy mysteries. She lives in "The Granite State" with her husband, two sons, two cats and lovable Labradoodle.

When she isn't working on her stories she likes to tend to her flowers, relax with her pets and play video games with her family.

Get in Touch with Wendy
www.wendymeadows.com

amazon.com/author/wendymeadows

goodreads.com/wendymeadows

bookbub.com/authors/wendy-meadows

facebook.com/AuthorWendyMeadows

twitter.com/wmeadowscozy

Made in the USA
Monee, IL
15 September 2021